THE
RAIN CITY
HUSTLE

ALSO BY
M.D. GRAYSON
Danny Logan Mystery Series
ANGEL DANCE

NO WAY TO DIE

ISABEL'S RUN

MONA LISA EYES

BLUE MOLLY

THE RAIN CITY HUSTLE

... move fast, stay one step ahead.

by

M.D. GRAYSON

cedar coast press

Copyright © 2022 by M.D. Grayson

Copyright

🌲 **cedar coast press**

Published by Cedar Coast Press, LLC
www.cedarcoastpress.com

This book is a work of fiction. Names, characters, places, and incidents are either the product of the author's imagination or are used fictitiously. Any resemblance to actual persons, living or dead, or to actual events or locales is entirely coincidental.

THE RAIN CITY HUSTLE
Copyright © 2022 by M.D. Grayson

All rights reserved including the right to reproduce this book, or portions thereof, in any form. No part of this text may be reproduced, transmitted, downloaded, decompiled, reverse-engineered, or stored in or introduced into any information storage and retrieval system, in any form or by any means, whether electronic or mechanical, without the express written permission of the author. The scanning, uploading, and distribution of this book via the Internet or via any other means without the permission of the publisher is illegal and punishable by law. Please purchase only authorized editions and do not participate in or encourage piracy of copyrighted materials.

Cover design by M.D. Grayson
Licensed cover art:
Copyright © Adobe Stock # 206226674 Horse Racing Watercolor by Yulia
Copyright © Adobe Stock # 198583881 Vector Water Drops on Glass by Oleh

First Edition: September 2022
Ver. 09152022

ISBN—EBook 979-8-986-2907-0-6
ISBN—Paperback 979-8-9862907-1-3
ISBN—Hardback 979-8-986-2907-2-0

10 9 8 7 6 5 4 3 2 1

To Carol Mazzeo
... move fast, stay one step ahead

THE
INVESTIGATORS

CHAPTER 1

Midnight at Hunts Point

The tall cedar trees on the sloping grounds of the majestic Hunts Point home swayed back and forth in the moonlight, moving to the warm night wind like sensuous dancers, casting long wavy shadows across the expansive, carefully manicured lawn. Within these dark, undulating shapes, Seattle private investigator Danny Logan silently made his way up the incline, dashing from one shadow to the next, pausing briefly here and there to make sure he'd not been discovered, then moving on. One hundred yards from the shore, he ducked behind a tall rhododendron and carefully parted the branches.

Ahead, perhaps another fifty yards up the slope, a low brick wall with wrought-iron pickets marked the top of the rise. Beyond the wall, a huge home lay shrouded in darkness—quiet, dimly lit, the outline barely visible.

Danny took his time and scanned the building and the

grounds. Glancing back, he could see the waters at the eastern edge of Lake Washington lapping quietly against the shore. Three miles across on the lake's far western side, the lights of Seattle cast reflections that shimmered all the way across the surface, rippling in rhythm with the waves. A dark hole in the lights near the water's edge marked the spot where a jet-black Zodiac Hurricane inflatable waited for him, engines idling. At the helm was a lone darkened figure—a woman, dark hair flowing in the gentle wind. Toni Blair, Danny's business partner and fiancée, watched the home and the grounds through the green lenses of night-vision goggles while the small boat's powerful twin engines gurgled softly, barely audible above the crickets and the breeze whistling through the trees.

The sound of the boat's engines was further masked by a rhythmic *thump-thump-thump* of a hip-hop tune coming from ahead up the slope. Danny studied the source of the music—the estate's guest house—a small cottage offset from the main house and situated just below the brick wall near a walkway that led all the way down to the water and a large boat dock.

In stark contrast to the quiet main house, the guest cottage was alive with activity. Lights spilled out through a sliding glass patio door, rolled across the deck, and then washed over the lawn. Loud voices came from inside the house—laughing, yelling.

Danny continued to study the guest house a moment longer before the earpiece he wore crackled to life with Toni's voice. "It's noisy up there."

"Yeah. How 'm I looking?" he whispered into the microphone at the end of his earpiece.

"You're clear. You sure you still want to do this?"

"Yeah—got to. I promised Kate." He paused. Then, looking up at the main house, he added, "You were right—this place is something."

"Told ya. Frank Thorne's doing all right for himself."

"Sure is." A moment later, he said, "Okay, I'm moving." With a final look around to make sure all was clear, he started to take a step forward when suddenly he froze.

He slid back into the shadows. "One other thing—almost forgot. What about the dogs? You said the boys saw dogs this afternoon."

"I did. But not now. You're clear . . . still."

Danny furrowed his brow. "Still?" he mouthed, raising an eyebrow. He waited a moment, then he moved out. He sprinted up and across the yard to his left, making a beeline for the corner of the guest-house deck, deviating slightly only to avoid the areas of lawn illuminated by the lights from the party. Ten seconds later, he reached the safety of the shadows and ducked alongside the building. While he caught his breath, he waited and listened. No alarm, no dogs.

The layout of the guest house and deck was simple—a small L-shaped building wrapped around a wood-planked deck oriented toward the lake. A steaming hot tub dominated the middle of the deck and was flanked by a table with a folded umbrella and a couple of wooden chairs. Two sliding glass doors opened onto the deck from the house—one from each side of the L. Both were closed. The room behind the first slider was dark, the window covered with curtains. The other glass door appeared to lead to the small home's brightly lit living room. It was not covered.

Danny glanced upward and noted a single security camera on the eave, but it was mounted directly above him and aimed at the hot tub. It should not be a factor. He stepped over the low rail and swung himself up onto the deck. Pressed against the wall to stay out of camera view, he began a stealthy shimmy toward the living room slider. At the edge of the door, he paused for a moment. He took a breath, then he stole a very quick glance inside. No one there. An empty champagne bottle sat on the coffee table alongside an ashtray full of cigarette butts. Although the music still played, he no longer heard any voices. He ducked back behind the wall.

Hidden in the shadows, he tilted his head and pursed his lips. A moment later, he shrugged and shook his head. Then he took another look, slower this time—more careful, more deliberate.

Still no one there.

Peering around the edge of the door, Danny began scanning the room from left to right, one segment at a time. Halfway through, he froze when he spotted a large oil painting resting on an easel in a corner of the room, perched like an information poster in a hotel lobby. He stared at the brilliant orange, yellow, and blue painting, barely breathing. This was no hotel poster.

"It's here!" he whispered into the radio, his eyes still fixed on the painting. "It's right here—right where she said it would be, right out in the open, not more than fifteen feet away."

"Good. Now you can tell Kate. Take a picture, and then let's get out of here."

"Roger."

"Make sure your flash is off."

He smiled, but still he double-checked before he grabbed a picture with his phone. He continued to stare at the painting, studying the masterpiece, his head tilted first one way, then the other. After a long minute, he started to turn away at the very instant the motor on the hot tub behind him suddenly burst to life with a low scream like a jet's turbine engine. The steaming water began to boil with bubbles.

He fumbled his phone, snatched it out of midair, then jumped sideways, back into the shadows, where he flattened himself against the wall. Almost immediately, the music inside the guest house clicked off, and the night fell silent, save for the whine of the hot tub. The bedroom glass door began to slide open. Danny froze, barely breathing, his muscles tensed.

A moment later, someone inside pushed the heavy blackout drapes aside, revealing the corner of a bed. Bright lights spilled out onto the deck, illuminating the hot tub and half the deck—fortunately the half on the other side of the hot tub, away from Danny. A shapely leg appeared, then a short young woman with long blond hair stepped outside.

She wore a scanty white bikini, barely more than a collection of strategically placed strings. In her hand was a half-full champagne flute. The young woman took a couple of tentative steps, wobbling slightly, her empty hand extended as she tried to find her equilibrium. She steadied for a moment, seemed to sniff the air, then took another unsteady step forward. The movement was apparently too abrupt for her, and again, she started to lose her balance. She lurched toward the doorpost behind her and spilled her champagne on the deck.

"Oops!" she said, giggling, grabbing on to the post and swaying, sloshing champagne on the rail.

She caught her balance and looked up—directly at a frozen-in-place Danny. He was in full stealth mode, dressed in black, from his dark trail-running shoes to his stocking cap. Even his face was painted with black and green camo grease. He remained completely motionless, holding his breath.

The young woman stared for a moment, but her eyes had not yet fully adjusted to the dark. She turned away and, gathering herself, took a few lurching steps toward the deck rail facing Lake Washington, opposite Danny. When she reached the safety of the rail, she braced herself and stared at the lights. A minute later, she leaned forward and threw her arms wide in a classic I'm-the-queen-of-the-world-Kate-Winslet-on-the-bow-of-the-*Titanic* pose, her long hair flowing in the breeze. She breathed deeply of the night air. Then she called out, "Billy! Come here. You gotta see this. It's awesome!"

Danny shifted his gaze back to the door and shook his head slowly. "No, you don't, Billy," he whispered. He started to slink toward the rail and escape, but then a new noise came from inside the bedroom, a quiet *tap-tap-tap* behind the curtain. He froze again.

"Come on, Billy!" she called out.

"I'll be there in a minute," a man answered from inside. "I've seen them lights a million times." The tapping resumed. "Hey, I'm cuttin' some lines here. You want one?"

The woman didn't answer, her attention captured by the lights.

"Chloe!"

"What?" She paused, then said, "Oh yeah. 'Course I do." She turned around and took a step toward the door, and this time, her eyes now acclimated to the dark, she saw Danny.

She stopped and rocked backward, then forward, her eyes wide, mouth open. She wobbled slightly and struggled to make sense of the dark shape hiding in the shadows before her.

Danny remained still for a couple of seconds, but when the young woman took another step toward him, he slowly raised his finger to his lips.

She gasped and stopped, but she didn't cry out. Danny smiled. Nodding slowly, as if to reassure her, he started to take a side step toward the rail. This broke her trance, and an instant later, the young woman let loose a blood-curdling scream that shattered the quiet night.

* * * *

Danny was airborne before the scream was done echoing off the main house. He easily vaulted the deck rail but landed hard in the soft dirt of a planter, where he stumbled and sprawled forward on his hands and knees on the lawn. He recovered quickly, though, and burst into a sprint down the hill, toward the water. He'd taken only a few steps when he heard the unmistakable *RACK!* of a pump-action shotgun being cocked from close behind him.

"Damn!" He zigged hard to his left, toward the shadows, just as a huge divot in the lawn exploded into the air not more than a yard to his right, accompanied by a deafening *BOOM!*

"Stop!"

"Like hell!" he gasped. He zigged again, this time to the right. Another loud *RACK! BOOM!* followed, along with another piece of exploding turf, this one to his left and not quite so close.

His radio crackled to life. "You need help?"

"No! Be ready to go!"

He raced down the middle of the hill, weaving wildly in a random fashion as the shots continued sporadically.

Halfway to the boat, near the rhodie bush where he'd paused on the way up the hill, the shots stopped. "I think . . . I'm okay," he gasped into the radio, slowing slightly.

Then he heard the dogs. "Uh-oh!"

"You need help?" Toni said again.

"No! Wait there!"

He leaned into his sprint with renewed vigor as the barking dogs quickly drew closer. Seconds later, lungs bursting, he reached the bottom of the slope and sailed over the seawall, landing on the soft gravel beach without the slightest stumble or buckle this time. The dogs were close enough that he could hear them panting. Danny shot across the beach in three long strides and hit the water with an awkward splash just as the dogs flew over the seawall.

He took two giant floundering steps in the dark lake water and then hurled himself clumsily over the boat's inflatable side tube, landing hard on the fiberglass floor of the forward deck. Behind him, the dogs skidded to a halt at the water's edge, barking furiously. Danny turned to Toni. "Go! Go! Go!"

Toni slammed the throttles forward, and the boat shot backward away from the shore. Fifty yards out, she throttled back for an instant and shifted into forward. "Hang on!" She spun the wheel hard to starboard and shoved the throttles full forward again. The small boat nearly leaped completely out of the water as it spun around and sped away to the west, soon disappearing into the night.

CHAPTER 2

Fade to Crimson

The morning dew had yet to burn off the cherry laurels fronting the Chihuly Garden and Glass exhibit at Seattle Center when Danny and Toni walked toward a line of low white barriers. The barriers were connected to one another by shiny yellow tape emblazoned with the words POLICE LINE DO NOT CROSS that surrounded a circular area extending from the museum all the way to the Space Needle and back.

"That way," Danny said, yawning. He nodded toward an opening in the barriers.

Toni glanced at him. "You need a nap already?"

"After last night? Probably."

"Better suck it up, old man."

Within the cordoned-off space, a dozen men worked at moving a small mountain of lighting, sound, and camera equipment, wheeling dollies, and pushing loaded carts from two large trailers. The gear was being assembled under the careful direction of a young woman with bushy auburn hair gathered in a loose ponytail. "No, not there!" she said to one of the men. "Look, Brian—pay attention! There's already a shadow on that door." She pointed to a spot five feet left of where the man had just set up a light stand. "Light's gotta go over *there* so it washes the door."

"Is that Kate?" Toni asked.

Danny shook his head. "No. I don't know who that is. I—"

"Hey!" A voice behind them interrupted him. "We don't let just anyone in here!"

Danny jumped as he spun around. A rotund, silver-haired Seattle PD officer stood guard at the entry next to a sign that read:

FADE TO CRIMSON
CLOSED SET
AUTHORIZED PERSONS ONLY

The cop had a wide grin on his face.

Danny broke into a smile and chuckled. "Eddie G! You scared the hell out of me."

"Hiya, Eddie!" Toni said. She leaned forward and hugged the short, round policeman.

Eddie embraced her, then stepped back. "Oh, boy! Now we gotta watch out! Logan PI is in the house!"

"Darn straight," Toni said. "And don't you forget it!"

"Never!" He lowered his voice. "Actually, I knew you were coming. Kate told me to watch out for a couple of tall, good-lookin' PIs, so I been on the lookout. And now here you are! You're good-lookin'—he's tall!"

Toni laughed. "Don't kid yourself, shorty. I'm taller than you."

Eddie sucked in his gut and stood up straight. "That ain't sayin' much, doll."

Danny shook Eddie's hand and glanced around. "Doing some moonlighting, huh, Eddie?"

Eddie nodded. "You bet. It's easy money: Kate says, 'Public stays on that side of the line, crew stays on this side of the line.'" He shrugged. "I can do that." He paused, then he reached into a folder sitting on a nearby chair. "They made up some set passes for you two. Keep you from having one of the other guys giving you the toss."

"Thanks."

"No sweat, man," Eddie said. "Say—I bumped into the lieutenant yesterday. He told me to tell you hello. He says wedding bells are fixin' to ring for you two."

"Word gets around." Danny said.

"Around here it does, you lucky dog."

Toni beamed. "I finally got him tied down. Third time's the charm."

Danny glanced at her. "Finally tied down? Yeah, right. For the record, all the delays have been a *mutual* decision. We—"

"No!" A woman nearby raised an angry voice, cutting him off. Thirty feet away, in front of a row of three trailers parked beside the equipment trailers, the woman and a man were arguing.

"No!" she said again. "We cannot change this part of the schedule again, Ray!" She glared at the man, motionless.

"Oh, boy. Here they go again," Eddie said, his voice lowered. Danny leaned over and whispered to Toni, "*That's* Kate."

Toni nodded. "I see. And the poor guy getting lit up?"

"I'm not sure. That would appear to be Ray, the boyfriend she told me about."

"That's Ray, all right," Eddie said.

"This happen a lot?"

"The fight? Let's just say the two of them been havin' their fair share of what you might call 'creative disagreements' here lately."

The argument continued, Kate and Ray furious with each other. Finally, after Kate emphasized a point by poking Ray in the chest, Toni rolled her eyes. "We'd better go separate them before Eddie has to ring them up for domestic violence."

* * * *

"And besides, you know good and well that you're in no position to be making demands." Kate's voice was lower now, but no less resolute.

Ray's face dropped. "That's not fair and you know it."

"Yeah? It is what it is. Fair or not, deal with it." She leaned forward. "Production's running late and getting later, and for some strange reason, you don't seem to give a rat's rear end." She paused, then she tilted her head. "Speaking of which, you never did say why you cut out early yesterday. Where were you? Murphy had to step in and take over. Again."

"You know where I was. I had a meeting with the new editor, an interview."

"All that time?"

"It went longer than I thought. We had a lot to go over. Besides, yesterday's shot was simple, and Murphy knows what she's doing. It's not a big deal. I'll get us back on track—we just need a few more days. We'll be better than ever. And reshooting today's scene over at the stadium won't take more than—"

"Stop!" Kate held up her hand. "We are *not* reshooting the scene over at the stadium!" She leaned in even farther.

Kate was in her early thirties with long, dark hair. She wasn't exactly short, but Ray was basketball-player tall, so the closer she leaned in, the more she had to tilt her face upward. "Look around you. We paid good money to get a permit to film here. The rental meter for the space and for all the gear is ticking away. If you screw this schedule up, that means the setup is wasted, the permit is wasted, all this"—she waved her arms toward the set—"all this will be wasted. We won't get finished shooting on time, and then we'll be in trouble. Big trouble." She paused. "You do remember what that means, right?"

Ray stared back, his mouth clenched shut.

"Right?" Kate repeated.

Ray still said nothing, so Kate continued. "So, you *make* it work, Ray. Just like it is. Make. It. Work."

The stare-down lasted another five seconds or so, then Ray folded, his shoulders drooping. He pursed his lips and blew out slowly, then he nodded. "Okay, sure. We'll do it your way. Again." He gave her a thin smile. "We always do it your way, right, Kate?

So we'll do it your way this time, too. But I'm telling ya, the film won't be as good." He glared at her for a final moment, then he spun around and marched off toward the set.

"Let's go!" he shouted to the crew, several of whom stood nearby, pretending not to watch. Then, more angrily, "What are you all doing standing around? Let's get back to work!" He paused. Then, glancing back at Kate, he barked, "Meter's running!"

Kate watched for a second, taking several deep breaths before she turned and noticed Danny and Toni standing nearby, holding back at a discreet distance. She rolled her eyes, then she grimaced and walked over. "I'm sorry you guys had to see that little . . . disagreement."

"No problem," Danny said. "Just like old times, right? Kickin' ass, takin' names."

Kate rolled her eyes. "Yeah, I suppose." She shook her head. "Worked better in the army. Didn't know I'd be having to do it with the guy who's supposed to be my partner."

"Kate Morgan," he said, "I'd like you to meet my fiancée and business partner, Toni Blair."

Kate reached for Toni's hand. "Toni, it's nice to meet you. Danny told me about you yesterday." She smiled. "'Course he left out the part about you looking like a model, though." She turned and gave Danny's sleeve a tug. "Then again, he is a man of few words, right?" Turning back to Toni, she said, "He tell you we were in the army at the same time? In Iraq?"

"He did."

"We were buddies. We watched out for each other, had each other's back."

Danny nodded. "That's true."

Kate smiled, then she playfully slugged Danny in the arm. Before he could respond, she turned back to Toni and continued. "So, I don't know what he told you, but I hadn't seen this guy here in, like, I don't know, ten, twelve *years*, not since his deployment ended, and he rotated back, and they turned him into an army cop. Then, yesterday morning, out of the blue, I'm walking out of Starbucks, and I literally bump right into him—after all that time! Almost dumped my latte on his shirt." She smiled. "Sergeant Logan, in the flesh. We used to . . ." Suddenly, the smile left her face. "Last night?"

Danny glanced around. "You think there might be a place we could sit down for a few minutes in private? I gave Toni the rundown on what we talked about yesterday, but she has some questions. Now a good time?"

Kate pointed toward the trailers. "Yeah, you bet. I've got a conference call with the bankers at ten, but that gives us an hour or so. I'm in the middle rig there."

* * * *

Kate's production trailer was a mobile office with a desk and a small conference table. Two telephones and a fax machine were perched on a small kitchen counter. "Okay," Kate said, "I'll hit the highlights, then you can fire away with questions. Ray and I own the world's smallest independent film company. Well, technically, *I* own it, but we run it together. We're here near the end of the production phase of our third film, *Fade to Crimson*. It's a murder mystery set here in Seattle. We're shooting a few scenes here at the Space Needle now. A couple of months ago, Ray offered to run over to my father's condo in Bellevue. He has a place on a lake in Italy where he spends the summer, but he's got a small army of people who take care of his condo here while he's gone—maids, window cleaners, houseplant keepers, and the like. Once a month, he wants me to check up on them— make sure no one stole the silverware, mooched his Scotch, that sort of thing. Knowing my father, he's probably got someone checking up on me, too." She smiled. "Sort of a 'super checker.' Anyway, that particular day, I was slammed, so I said, 'Sure, honey, that'd be great if you could do that for me.'"

She gave a broad theatrical smile. "So thoughtful, right?" She paused for an instant, and the smile disappeared. "Nope. Not even close to right. I should've known better. Turns out that while he was there 'picking up the mail,' Ray was also planning to do a little corporate financing. All of a sudden, he was worried about the company's financial position, so he figured it'd be a swell idea to swipe a very expensive oil painting right off Dad's living room wall, which he then proceeded to take downstairs past the bellman and right out the front door. They'd seen him before with me, so no one even thought to ask what he was doing. Without saying anything to me, he turned the painting over as collateral for a loan that we may or may not need in order to finish our film. His bright idea was to finish the film, get our next round of funding, then pay off the loan and get the painting back on the wall before anyone noticed. Including me."

She smiled. "I run the finances, and we *were* running a little tight, but c'mon! I had it under control, more or less. Of course, Ray knew what I'd have said if he'd run this genius scheme of his past me, so naturally, he kept his mouth shut."

"Danny showed me the picture of the painting," Toni said. "*Lys dans de Champs de Moret—Lilies in the Fields of Moret.*"

"That's the one. Alfred Sisley. 1887."

"I looked it up yesterday afternoon. It's beautiful. It must be worth a fortune."

Kate nodded. "It is. A small fortune, anyway. It's an Impressionist piece. Not like a Monet, but valuable, for sure. My father paid two million for it three years ago. No doubt it's gone up in value since then."

Toni's eyes opened wide. "Whoa! That *is* a fortune. Your dad's a collector?"

Danny nodded. "Did I mention Kate's dad is Taylor Morgan?"

She glanced at Danny and raised an eyebrow. "Morgan? Bellevue shopping centers Taylor Morgan?"

Danny nodded. "Yep."

She stared at him a moment, then she gave him an amused smile and shook her head. "No, you forgot to say anything about that."

"Sorry. But, yeah, that's him—Bellevue shopping centers. Wait, though, it gets better."

"Okaaay."

Kate continued. "Right. So Ray plays cute. To keep the deal hidden from me, he puts the loan money in a separate account that he opens and doesn't tell me about. Shame on me, I noticed that the bills weren't coming through at the same pace, but I thought that the vendors were just slow with their invoices. Like I said, funds were starting to get a little scarce, so I wasn't going to complain." She shook her head. "Turns out the bills weren't late after all. Ray was intercepting them and paying some of them out of his secret account, and that's why I never saw them." She shrugged. "I'm embarrassed to say that I never caught on—I didn't know anything about Ray's arrangement."

"How'd you find out?"

Kate smirked. "How'd I find out. Three weeks ago, I'm over on the set, and these two gangster-looking dudes walk up, acting like they own the place or something. They had set passes, and at first I thought they were extras Ray had brought in without telling me. They looked the part, and spending money on extras without telling me is something Ray's pretty good at."

"Let me guess," Toni said. "One of those guys was Billy Thorne."

"You got it. There were two of them. He was the younger one, but he was in charge, you know? The other guy didn't say a word. Anyway, Thorne was all dressed up in black, got his hair all slicked back, he's got this attitude, all puffed up. He looks like a vampire from *Twilight* or something. He comes up to me, and he goes all Tony Soprano and says, 'Hey, babe, Ray says you control the purse strings around here. I'm wonderin' when you're gonna pay me back.'"

She shrugged. "I had no idea who this clown was or what he was talking about. At first, I actually thought it was some kind of a strange way of hitting on me. So I told him to take a hike. He laughed, but they left. Afterward, I mentioned it to Ray. Damn if he doesn't start getting all twitchy, like he knew! I could see it on his face! I said, 'What the hell, Ray?' He hemmed and hawed for a bit, but he finally came clean. He said he thought we were tight and that he'd been given the name of a guy concerning a loan—Billy Thorne. So he met with him. Ray doesn't have much in the way of good judgment, but any that he did have all flew out the window when he met Thorne. Ray said Thorne said he'd make the loan and when he met him for their second meeting, Thorne proceeded to open up a duffel bag with five hundred thousand dollars cash in it. Ray was a goner."

"Whoa," Toni said. "*Big* cash! I can see where that could have been tempting."

"I guess that was Thorne's point. Shouldn't have worked, but whatever, it was too much for Ray to turn down."

"So Billy Thorne gives five hundred grand to Ray, who then turns over your father's two-million-dollar painting as collateral?"

"Yep. Five hundred thousand dollars, plus interest. They want a hundred thousand bucks for a ninety-day loan."

"Geez," Toni said, taking a deep breath and blowing it out slowly. She glanced at Danny. "With those kinds of rates, I guess that's how Frank Thorne ends up with the big house on the water."

"It would seem," Danny said, nodding.

"Oh, it gets worse," Kate said, rolling her eyes. "Late last week, Thorne shows up again. This time, I knew who he was, so I was better prepared. I told him we were close to being able to pay him back, but we might need an extension—a month or so—and that we'd be willing to pay for it, another twenty-five grand. He doesn't even give it a thought. He immediately says, 'We don't do extensions.' Then he drops the big bomb. He's like, 'But don't worry about it. You don't have to bother about paying me back at all.' That was a surprise, so I say, 'Why's that?' And he says he'll forgive the loan in exchange for the painting—says he's got it set up in his living room, and he likes it. Plus, he says he's also got a buyer lined up who wants to pick it up right away."

Kate narrowed her eyes. "I couldn't believe it. I was floored. But it gets worse. Before I could answer, he says that if that particular buyer falls through, he even has a backup plan—he's going to take it to an auction in New York next month. Either way, I don't have to worry about paying the loan back. When I could finally function again, I told him to hold on. I wasn't interested in letting him have my father's painting and that he could forget about selling it. We had until September 16, and we'd definitely be paying him back."

"What'd he say?"

"He laughed. He said, 'Don't be late.' Then they left." Kate sat back and took a deep breath and let it out slowly. She looked at Danny, then back at Toni. "I don't know exactly where things are at now, but it's looking pretty obvious to me like Thorne's done the math. He knows what the painting's worth. Ray was stupid enough to turn it over, and now Thorne doesn't want to give it back. He wants to keep it and sell it for big bucks, and I'm afraid he's gonna play every angle he can to make it happen. Not that he has to, with this ticking time bomb running. If we miss our payoff deadline by ten minutes, he automatically gets the painting, and it's game over anyway. So we can't have any more delays." She rolled her eyes. "Which is a problem since Ray's the director, and he considers himself an 'artist.' He wouldn't know a schedule if it jumped up and bit him in the ass, which is why I have to ride him constantly."

"You think you can make it happen?" Toni asked.

Kate took a quick breath. "It's gonna be close. Our next round of funding, which would be our post-production loan, is already arranged. But *post*-production means *after* we're done filming. It's doable. But things have to go right."

Toni glanced at Danny, then she turned to Kate. "Kate, I gotta ask the obvious. I mean, your father's, like, a gozillionaire, right? Why not just ask him for the money? Protect the painting. Pay off Thorne right now and remove the heat. Then, later on, use your normal financing to pay your dad back. Problem solved."

Kate smiled. "I may have forgotten to mention that my father knows nothing about this little calamity—nor can he ever. You guys don't know him, but take my word for it, he's not the most understanding man in the world. If he *ever* found out what Ray's done—and that means me too, by association—there'd be this gigantic shift in the space-time continuum. Ray would get to spend the next several years in the state penitentiary, which, despite our current problems, is not something I'd wish on him. And my relationship with my father—admittedly not always the best—would essentially come to a shattering end." She shook her head. "*I* need to solve this. Bringing my father in is not something I'm inclined to do."

"Fair enough," Toni said.

"Besides, this is fixable. We can pull the next financing off, as long as Ray sticks to the schedule. And as long as Billy Thorne actually gives us the time."

Danny pursed his lips. "Sorry to hear all this, Kate, but I do have some good news." He pulled out his phone and held it up so she could see the photo of the painting.

Kate glanced at him, then her eyes widened. "You found it?"

"Yeah. Thorne might have a buyer arranged, as he claims—no way to tell. But as of last night, anyway, the painting was definitely still in his possession. It's sitting in his living room all right, just like he said it was."

Kate started to smile, then she turned and slugged Danny in the arm. "I can't believe you! You let me sit here all this time, sweating this thing out, and you didn't say anything? Why didn't you call me when you found out?"

"At two a.m.? Here, I'll send you the picture."

She exhaled sharply with relief. "Thank God for that. Maybe we still have a shot." Kate looked from Danny to Toni. "So, now that you two have heard the whole story, is this the kind of thing you guys work with? Helping people get out of jams like this? You think you could help?"

"We've never actually worked with someone in a jam like this before," Danny said. "And I'm honestly not sure what we can do. Ray's put you in a tough spot, but although a bad business deal might not be very smart, it's not necessarily illegal. About all you can do is get the funds together and pay him off."

"He can't sell it, though, right?"

"No," Toni said. "He has to give you the time you guys

agreed to. Danny's dad's a lawyer. One thing we *can* do is talk to him, ask him what he thinks. Maybe he could send a letter to Thorne, ask for an extension. At least demand that you get the time promised."

Kate nodded.

"Meanwhile," Danny said, "we could do a little digging around on our own as well, see what we can find."

* * * *

"It's happening again, isn't it?" Toni said. She and Danny were stuck in traffic on the way back to their office.

"No, it's not." Danny stared straight ahead, eyes on the road.

Toni glanced over at him. "You don't even know what I'm talking about."

Danny smiled. "We've been together seven years. —I know what you're *thinking* even if you don't say it. You think the wedding's going to get pushed back. Again."

"Well?"

"Not happening."

"This is how it starts, though. A big job comes up, something we can't ignore."

Danny said nothing.

"What about your army buddy? What if she needs our help?"

Danny raised an eyebrow, took a deep breath, let it out slowly. Then he shook his head. "Trust me. No more postponements. We're getting married on September 12, as scheduled. Period."

Toni looked at him a moment longer, then she turned and stared straight ahead.

CHAPTER 3

Keeping Up With the Joneses

Billy Thorne rolled over and saw that Chloe had already left. He glanced at the clock on the nightstand—ten minutes after eleven a.m. Yawning, he got up and splashed a little water on his face before running a comb through his dark hair and throwing on his standard summer-morning-after-a-hard-night outfit—bathing suit, straw hat, dark glasses, flip-flops, and a robe. He left the guest house, not bothering to lock the door, and began to shuffle up the gardeners' path that snaked around the rhododendrons toward the pool deck and the main house.

As he drew near, he paused when he heard splashing and laughing coming from the pool. He listened intently. *Someone* was having a good time, and the *someone* sounded female, or, more correctly, *females*. He smiled and continued on his way, his pace a little quicker now.

Billy rounded the final corner, stepped onto the brick pool deck, and immediately stopped. He was right! Two attractive young women *were* playing in the pool, laughing and splashing each other. Billy soaked in the vision for a long moment before continuing, taking his time, stealing glances as he ambled over to a poolside table shaded by a large, colorful umbrella.

A bald man was seated at the table, his back to the pool. His biceps bulged beneath a tight-fitting, bright red Manchester United jersey. The man was reading *The Seattle Times*, an orange juice before him, the glass sweating in the humid air. Billy took the seat across from him and shifted his chair to ensure a good view of the swimmers.

"Morning, Nigel." He looked toward the pool. "Don't see that every day. Who're your friends?"

Nigel slid a large michelada over to him without looking up. "Good morning to you." His voice carried a distinct northern British accent.

"Thanks." Billy nodded toward the girls again. "So?"

Nigel lifted his eyes and looked at him, his brow furrowed. "The blond *youngster* there in the blue bikini is Miss Jordan Perkins, as in Lorraine's *daughter* Jordan Perkins." He paused for a moment, then added, "Notice how I stressed the words 'youngster' and 'daughter'?"

Billy continued to stare. "Yeah, I caught that. The other?"

"The other young lady is Jordan's friend whose name . . . whose name escapes me at the moment."

Billy admired the girls for a second, then he turned to Nigel. "So *that's* Lorraine's daughter?"

Nigel gave a quick nod. "Yep."

Billy took a slow deep breath. "She doesn't look all *that* young."

Nigel's eyes narrowed slightly. "Doesn't matter. She's *Lorraine's* daughter."

"Yeah, you said that." Billy watched the girls for another few moments, then he shrugged. "Too bad." He reached for the michelada and took a long pull. "Ahhh," he said, leaning back in his chair. He closed his eyes for a moment and pressed the cool glass against his forehead. "Better." A minute later, he nodded toward the main house. "So, if the daughter's down *here*, I suppose that means Lorraine's up *there*?"

"Good guess. She's inside. With your father."

Billy grimaced. "Wonderful."

"Careful now. You may well be talking about your soon-to-be stepmum."

Billy yawned. "Don't remind me." He paused, then added, "She doesn't like me, you know. Thinks I'm lazy. Shiftless."

"A misread if ever I heard one."

Billy glanced at him, eyes narrowing. "Wiseass. Misunderstood? Maybe. Misappreciated . . . underappreciated? Definitely." He knocked back another slug of his drink. "Doesn't matter. I'm going to fix all those little misconceptions when we sell that painting next month. Once and for all. No more crap from Lorraine." He stared at the pool for a several seconds, then he said, "Anyway, I thought the old man spent the night at her place in the city last night."

"He did. They got home a little while ago." Nigel paused,

then said, "Fair warning—I'm told he's quite upset."

"Yeah?" Billy shrugged. "So what's new?"

"At you."

"Again, what's new?"

Nigel reached into a small bag on the table and pulled out five red empty shotgun shells and placed them on the table. "Jog your memory a bit?"

Billy stared at the shells for a moment, then he chuckled. "Oh, that. I forgot about our intruder. Thanks for cleaning up."

Nigel nodded. "Me and Ernie and Theo took the boat and went looking for them. Didn't see a thing. And by the time we got back, your place was dark, so we didn't want to wake you. Am I correct in assuming that you didn't get a good look at the guy?"

Billy shook his head. "Nope. Chloe saw him on the deck, but it was dark. When I saw him, he had his back to me, running like a fool. Dude was fast, zigzagging like crazy. I almost fell into the hot tub trying to keep focused." He chuckled. "Probably scared the hell out of him, though."

"I imagine."

"I doubt he'll be back."

"Let's hope not."

Billy watched the girls for a moment before suddenly turning. "You're thinking the old man's pissed about last night?"

Nigel shrugged. "Something to consider, no?"

Billy thought for a moment, then his brow furrowed. "Something you're not saying?"

"Well, it's like this. You realize that your old man's trying to fit in, right? He wants these hoity-toity nobs around here to look at him the same way they look at all them megatech rock stars. Why do you think he's with Lorraine? Her looks?"

Billy stared at him for a moment, then he dramatically clutched at his heart. "You mean it's not true love?"

Nigel smiled. "Nice. But I didn't say that. Maybe . . . I don't know. But it ain't the only reason, that's for certain."

"Then why?" Billy shrugged. "She's not bad lookin', I suppose, not for someone her age." He turned to the girls in the pool. "Not as good as her daughter, though."

"It's not her looks, you twat. If all he wanted was looks, he could do like you—go get his own twenty-five-year-old gold digger, half Lorraine's age and half as smart. Easy. No strings and way cheaper, as long as you're careful." He leaned forward. "But it doesn't get him where he wants to go. Lorraine, though—she's old money. She's connected. He wants to be with her because she's legit."

"And he thinks that'll somehow rub off and make him legit, too? Good luck with that."

"Well, be that as it may . . ."

Billy shrugged. "Whatever. More power to him. He wants to play that game, have at it."

"So you *do* understand, then."

"Yes. Thank you for this morning's lesson. I get it."

Nigel stared at him for a moment. "Do ya really? 'Cause I don't think you're makin' the connection."

Billy scowled. "Well, excuse the hell out of me, then. Why don't you just get to the point?"

"Okay. Knowing your old man's motivations now, as you do,

how do you think he's going to feel about you banging away with your scatter-gun in the middle of the night? For that matter, when do you think was the last time *any* of these rich dudes around here broke out a twelve-gauge on Hunts Point? Probably not since the turn of the century—and by that, I mean the turn of the twentieth, not the twenty-first."

Billy stared, saying nothing.

"And to put a point on it," Nigel continued, "do you think your blasting away is going to help your old man get himself invited to the next round of poker and brandy on the next-door neighbor's yacht?"

Billy thought for a second, then he leaned forward and kept his voice low. "Nigel, if this is your way of delivering a long-winded ass-chewing on behalf of the old man for me trying to blow that guy away last night, you can save it. We had an *intruder*! A bad guy! Standing right there on my deck, not three feet away from my door—probably peekin' in my window and watching me and Chloe going at it!" Then, his voice rising, he said, "What would you have me do? Invite him in?"

"No, I would not," Nigel said, shaking his head. "And there's no need to get pissed at me. Since you went to the trouble of opening up on him, I kind of wish you'd've been sober so you could've at least winged him."

"Damn right," Billy said, his face reddened.

"But you weren't and you didn't. And besides, it doesn't matter what *I* like or don't like. I don't care, and I don't matter." He nodded toward the main house. "But *he* does."

Billy had been about to reach for the michelada to kill it

off, but he froze in place for an instant, then he slumped back in his chair and let out a heavy sigh. "Damn! This was gonna be a pretty good morning. Now I gotta go tell him what happened, don't I? Otherwise, Doyle or someone's gonna get to him first, if he already hasn't. He needs to hear it from me, or else he's gonna get all worked up and have my ass."

Nigel nodded slowly. "'Tween you and me, I think that would be an excellent idea."

Billy started to rise. "I'd better get on up . . ."

"Uh . . . Billy?"

Billy froze, suspended above his chair.

"Remember, Lorraine's here. You may want to get dressed first."

* * * *

Billy returned an hour later to find the pool area empty. As he approached the back door of the main house, showered and cleaned up, he caught his reflection in the tall glass windows.

He stopped, lifted up his sunglasses, and studied the image, posing, turning slightly one way, then the other. His dark hair was slicked back. He was dressed in black slacks and a black polo shirt. Satisfied, he smiled and lowered his Ray-Bans.

Inside the main house, the large gathering room facing the pool was empty. Billy crossed the room and tentatively knocked on the door to the study. A moment later, it swung open, and he was greeted by a sharply dressed, silver-haired man.

"Billy," the man said, his voice lowered.

"Doyle," Billy said, nodding curtly. He quickly scanned the room. His father was on the phone, seated behind a large desk. Lorraine Perkins sat on a nearby sofa, her pure blond hair pulled back tightly. She looked up from her *Town and Country* magazine, glanced at Billy, and almost succeeded in stifling a contemptuous sneer. Billy ignored her.

"Your dad's wrapping up a conversation," Doyle said as he closed the door behind Billy. "He'll be done in a minute. C'mon in."

Billy studied his father for a moment. Frank Thorne, just over sixty, was medium height and stocky, neither heavy nor slim, but muscular...powerful. His slicked-back hair was still full and mostly dark, although his sideburns were beginning to give way to gray. He wore a dark charcoal pinstripe suit with a crisp white shirt, gold cuff links and a striped burgundy tie. His coat hung on a hanger on a coat rack beside the door. He leaned forward in his chair, his face red with anger as he held the phone. He clenched the phone so tightly his knuckles were white.

"Blah, blah, blah! You listen to me, Andy!" he shouted into the phone. "I don't give a damn what his circumstances are. I want you to file those papers on him, and do it today! No more delays! Otherwise, it'll be *your* ass I'm comin' after!" A moment later, he said, "You make sure now, you got it?! Good!" He slammed the phone down and settled back in his seat.

He took a deep breath, blew it out slowly, then nodded at the two chairs in front of his desk. "Sit," he commanded. "Both of ya." He shook his head. "Try to run a legit business and my own damn lawyers are jerkin' us around." He made notes in a leather-covered notebook as Billy and Doyle took their seats.

A silent, uncomfortable full minute later, Frank laid his Montblanc pen on the desk and looked up. "Doyle, you follow up with those imbeciles this afternoon, ya hear? I want you to make absolutely certain they file the court papers. I want you to personally look at the court stamp with your own two eyes. I don't want any more excuses with this snivelin' little crybaby. Next thing, I'll be havin' Ernie and Theo pay him a little visit."

Doyle nodded. "Understood, boss."

"Good." Frank picked up the pen again and resumed writing. As he did so, he glanced at Billy. "What's up with you, Bill?"

Billy hesitated, then said, "Uh, Pop, I thought you should know that we had ourselves an intruder here last night."

Frank froze, his pen in midstroke. He slowly, deliberately capped the pen and set it down, then he leaned back in his chair. "What do you mean 'we had an intruder'?"

"I mean someone snuck onto the grounds and was standing outside my patio door last night—right up on my deck." He glanced at Doyle. "Doyle must have told you."

Frank ignored the last remark. "'Someone,' you say? We manage to catch this someone?"

Billy shook his head. "No. I . . ." He hesitated. "We tried. He got away."

"You see who it was?"

Billy shook his head again. "No, it was too dark out. We . . . scared him off, chased him. Turned the dogs out, even. But he got away."

"How'd he get away?"

"In a boat, if you can believe that. He ran down to the water's edge and took off in a boat, like some kind of Navy SEAL or something. Had someone waiting for him."

"On a boat." Frank pursed his lips and stared at Billy. After a few seconds, he took a deep breath. "He take anything?"

"No. Not that we can tell."

"We checked the house, Frank," Doyle added. "Nothin' seems to be missin'. Apparently, he didn't get near before Billy scared him off."

Frank turned to him. "So, you scared him off."

Billy nodded. "Sure did."

"But you didn't catch him. You didn't get a good look at him. And he didn't take nothin'," Frank mused. "You sure he was actually there? You sure you weren't a little loopy with that nose candy? Maybe you were seeing things? Maybe it was a ghost."

Billy shook his head. "No, no ghost, Pop. We saw him—I saw him. He was definitely there."

Frank took a deep breath and leaned back in his chair. "Didn't take nothin'. Didn't go to the main house . . ." His voice trailed off as he suddenly stood and turned and looked out a window that overlooked the backyard. A moment later, he turned back. "You geniuses consider maybe the house wasn't his target at all? Think about it. Guy's a pro, right? He's smart enough to sneak in from the water, yet he didn't come up to the big house, and he didn't take nothin'. But he *did* go to Bill's cottage. Maybe we should consider that that was no accident." He looked at the two, then added, "What's at the guest house that someone might be interested in?"

Billy sat upright. "Holy crap! He was after the painting!"

Frank pursed his lips and nodded slowly. "Brilliant."

"Son of a bitch," Doyle said, his voice trailing away.

Frank nodded. "Amazing, right?"

"Yeah."

"No, it's not!" Frank yelled, slapping the desk at the same time. Doyle and Billy both jumped. "It's freakin' obvious! And you two missed it!"

"The amazing thing," Lorraine said in a bored voice, "is that *Frank's* the one who's got to piece all this together. Geez."

Billy gave her a quick, nasty look, which she ignored as Frank smiled at her and said, "Thank you, dear." Then he turned back to Billy and Doyle. "She's right! *Of course* the guy was after the painting—*it's worth two million bucks!*" He turned to Billy. "This is *your* deal, Bill. You put it together. You're runnin' it. You wanted it, and it's got your name on it. But you should have anticipated something like this. You were sloppy. We got lucky this time—damn lucky. You shouldn't have an expensive painting just sittin' down there like it's at a friggin' yard sale! Hell, you probably don't even lock your doors."

"Sure I do," Billy lied.

Frank didn't respond. He took a deep breath, then said, "Got any ideas who it might have been?"

Billy shrugged. "If it's about the painting, then it's gotta be LeGrande. He's the obvious one. He and that girlfriend of his are the only ones that know we've got it. They want it back. I sure as hell didn't tell anyone else."

Frank rolled his eyes. "Ray LeGrande? Are you serious? You're saying that tall, skinny toothpick Ray LeGrande is going to sneak onto our property in the middle of the night in a speedboat and what? Steal the painting back?" He laughed. "What'd he do? Turn into Bruce Willis?"

Doyle shook his head. "Nah, LeGrande wouldn't try to steal it anyway. He wouldn't think he needed to. They're no doubt still planning to just pay off the loan and get the painting back, regular like."

Frank pursed his lips. "So who else could—" He stopped. Before anyone could answer, he answered himself. "It was an inside job."

"Inside?" Doyle's brow furrowed. "I don't know, boss, everybody around here's been checked out."

"Check 'em again! Maybe they didn't mean to rip it off themselves. Maybe they just talked. One big mouth—somebody who knows about this—that's all it takes. They start talkin' in front of the wrong guys, and now somebody else heard that we're sitting on a two-million-dollar painting over there in the living room of the damn cottage. Bam! They look at it like an engraved invitation. And next thing—what do you know?—we got a thief in the middle of the night."

"We should move it," Doyle said.

"You think? Get it up here to the vault right away."

Doyle nodded. "Done."

"And find Ernie and Theo. Tell them to double the guards on patrol—and tell 'em to pay attention, case the son of a bitch decides to come back for another try. No sense taking chances."

"Got it."

"And call the office. Let him know to beef up security over there, just in case."

"Got it."

"And I want you to call in Farley Palmer."

"Farley Palmer?" Billy asked. "The PI?"

Frank nodded. "Yeah, Farley Palmer. He's a pain in the ass, straight as a damn ruler, but he's good at what he does. He can find anything. Get him out here, have him look things over. Besides, we can use him to double-check the staff. Then I want to talk to him." He drew a deep breath, then he slowly shook his head. "I'll tell ya, word gets out that people can sneak out here and rip us off, we're in trouble."

He turned to Billy. "One other thing—just on the off-chance that you're right about Ray LeGrande. I want you to pay him a little visit. Take Nigel. And you may as well take Palmer, too, so he gets up to speed on what's going on. You put the fear of God into 'em, know what I mean?"

Billy nodded. "The girlfriend runs the show. She'll probably ask about an extension again, same as last time I was there."

Frank tilted his head. "You told her no, right?"

"Yeah, just like you said."

He shrugged. "Then what's the big deal? Tell her the same thing again."

"Okay." Billy turned to leave.

"Oh, Bill, there is one other thing."

Billy turned back. "Yeah?"

Frank drilled him with a hard, evil stare. "I ever hear about you firing a gun anywhere on this property again, I'm gonna take it and shove it up your dumb ass, ya got it?"

Billy looked at him for a second, then he looked at Lorraine. She smiled at him—a nasty, evil grin.

CHAPTER 4

Lis dans de Champs de Moret

Occidental Park at the south end of Seattle's Pioneer Square was crowded with late-afternoon visitors as Danny and Toni walked past. Children climbed on the bronze Fallen Firefighters Memorial statue while students seated at the bright yellow and green metal tables stared intently at their laptops. A pair of homeless men huddled together near the information booth, quietly sharing a cigarette.

"Hold up," Danny said just before they crossed Main Street. A surprisingly virtuoso classical guitar busker worked his way through a difficult passage of an intricate piece. "I know this song," he whispered. "It's a Segovia."

A couple of minutes later, the man finished.

"Well done," Danny said, dropping a ten-dollar bill into the man's worn guitar case. The musician nodded and started into his next number.

They crossed the street and walked to a tall, stately five-story brick building bearing a bronze nameplate that read Lyon Building. An art gallery was located on the ground floor at the corner. "Look," Toni said, pointing to a sign hanging inside the gallery's glass door that read "Lyon Gallery—By Appointment Only." She tried the door. It was locked. She peered inside. "That's funny, she knows we're coming. She—wait! *There* she is."

A moment later, a smartly dressed woman in her mid-forties unlocked and opened the door for them. "Hey! It's my two favorite detectives!"

"Sylvia!" Toni said as they stepped inside. "I'm so happy to see you." The two women hugged.

"Hey, Sylvia," Danny said, smiling broadly. "How are things?"

Sylvia shrugged. "Business is a little slow, but we're going to the big auction in New York next month. I have two drawings we're going to try and sell."

"Your own?"

"Yes. If we do well, it could make our whole year."

"That's exciting," Toni said. "Good luck!"

"Thanks," Sylvia said. "And how about you two? You're doing well?"

"We're good," Danny said. He nodded toward the sign. "What's with the locked door? You didn't used to do that, did you?"

Sylvia closed the door behind them and locked it again. "No. Nowadays, we don't have much of a choice. The homeless used to go to the missions at night. Now, though, there's so many that it seems the city's basically given up. They've given them all the parks plus some of the streets to camp on permanently. Just over on the other side of First Avenue there, it's wall-to-wall tent city. It's . . . it's . . . terrible."

She shook her head. "You sure can't walk over there. If we don't keep the doors locked, we have people wandering in all the time. And some of these people are so . . . so sad. They don't even know where they are."

"That's unfortunate," Toni said. "I'm sorry to hear it."

Sylvia nodded. "For us and for them."

"Gotta kill your walk-in traffic," Danny said.

Sylvia shrugged. "True. There's not so much of that now. The whole area is changing. People are staying away." She put her hand on Toni's arm. "But enough of that! I'm so excited! I got your wedding invitation, and you know we wouldn't miss it. Next month, right? The twelfth?"

Toni's eyes sparkled. "Yes. Can you believe it? One month from today. And it's actually going to happen this time."

"Perfect! The auction in New York is on the ninth, so we'll be back just in time."

"Good."

"So," Sylvia said, "why don't you two come on back?" She led the way to a small display room just off the main gallery floor that had been set up for private viewings with the gallery's patrons. "After we spoke on the phone, I put some information together for you," she said as they took seats around a small table.

"I must say I'm shocked—mortified, really—to hear that Taylor Morgan's Alfred Sisley might be at risk. What a tragedy! *Lys dans de Champs de Moret* is such a magnificent work." She opened a folder she'd prepared and slid each of them a color copy of the painting. "Just before you arrived, I emailed you each a copy of the painting. And here's a small print I made. *Lilies* is a truly special piece. I remember when Taylor acquired it. I was fortunate enough to see it in person. It's absolutely striking, a magnificent example of the Impressionist era." She studied the print for a moment, then she frowned. "And it's so very valuable. It would be horrible if anything bad were to happen to it."

Danny nodded. "We know. That's why we're trying to see what we can do to make sure that doesn't happen."

"You're working for Taylor?" Sylvia asked.

"His daughter, Kate. It's a . . . long story."

"Well, I'm happy to do what I can."

"You mentioned value," Toni said. "Kate said she thinks the painting's worth two million dollars, maybe more. Does this sound like a fair estimate to you?"

"Oh, I'd say that's conservative these days. I'm pretty sure that's about what Taylor paid for it three years ago. There's been significant movement in the fine art market since then. At the right auction in front of the right audience—like the Christie's auction next month, for instance—the painting might sell for much more than that today, maybe as much as double."

Toni raised her eyebrows. "Wow!"

"Indeed." Sylvia looked at one, then the other. "What happened? If you're at liberty to say."

Danny glanced at Toni, but she simply shrugged. "Go ahead."

"Well," he said, turning back to Sylvia, "without revealing too much confidential information, what I can say is that the painting was taken and given up as collateral for a business loan. Kate Morgan discovered it missing while her father has been away for the summer."

"She asked us to help get it back," Toni added, "preferably before her dad gets back from Europe."

"So Taylor is unaware?"

"That's correct. And Kate wants to keep it that way."

"I suppose I can understand that," Sylvia said. "But . . ." She hesitated. "I'm confused. How could anyone have gotten hold of the painting without proper authorization? The facility is supposed to be secure."

"Not so much," Danny said. "Somebody with an inside connection goes to take care of the condo, and they swipe the painting right off the wall and walk out the front door. Doorman's not really paying attention. Apparently, it wasn't that hard."

Sylvia considered this for a moment, then she suddenly sat straight up, her eyes opened wide. She held up her hand and leaned forward slightly. "You say that someone took the painting off the wall of Taylor's living room? From his condo in Bellevue?"

Danny nodded. "Yeah. Why?"

"No . . . no . . . wait." She rocked back, then a smile slowly spread across her face.

"What?" Danny said. "What is it?"

"Well, I'll be." She stood up. "I don't think Taylor's going to be too upset after all."

"Really?" Danny asked. "Why on earth not?"

"Because," she said, her eyes twinkling, "I'd be very willing to wager that the painting you're chasing—the one that came off the living room wall—it's not the original work. In fact, I'd venture to say it's not a painting at all: it's a copy."

Danny cocked his head and stared at her. "A copy?"

Sylvia nodded, smiling broadly. "Exactly. I think the painting from Taylor's condo is what is known in the trade as a display copy." She shook her head and let out a quick laugh. "Boy, I should have known when you first called, but I didn't realize ... You see, I've known Taylor Morgan for more than twenty years. He's a prolific art collector, very experienced. And I know one thing about him for certain: Taylor is a careful man. He knows full well that once a painting reaches a certain value, if it is to be displayed, it belongs in a museum. If not, it should be safely stored in a vault, a controlled environment, not hung on anyone's living room wall. These masterpieces are irreplaceable. Taylor knows this. He would *never* display such a valuable original on the wall of his home. Never. Far too risky, as you can see.

"Which is a problem, of course. One of the main reasons people invest in fine art in the first place is so that people can see it. The question then is how do you have your cake and eat it, too? The answer: When Taylor, or most serious collectors, buys an expensive piece, the very first thing he does after he takes delivery—*the very first thing*—is commission what's known as a display copy. Sometimes more than one. Then, once that's complete, he sends the original via armed guard to a secure facility specially designed for such purposes—all safe and sound, locked up in a climate-controlled vault that is safe from cigarette smoke, theft, fire, floods, UV damage even. Phew! My God, I thought when you called that somehow the *original Lilies* was gone. I couldn't figure out how someone could get to it."

Danny leaned back in his chair and took a deep breath,

blowing it out slowly. "A copy. Son of a bitch."

Toni said, "But I don't understand. The painting's been taken as collateral on a loan. How could that have happened if it's not real? Don't people check before they turn the money over? Aren't there, like, experts in the art world, people whose job it is to make sure the painting's real?"

"Oh, definitely. There's a whole industry dedicated to it."

"So how could it have slipped through—how could—"

Danny sat up straight, a half smile on his face. "It's simple. Because Billy Thorne didn't think that it might be fake, so he never had it verified. He saw what he wanted to see, and he left it at that. He was sloppy." He paused. "*If* this is what happened."

"It's easy enough to find out," Sylvia said, getting to her feet. "I think I know who Taylor most likely hired to copy it. Will Hollins—he's local. Everyone around here uses him. You can go on over and ask him yourself. Let me get his number." She left the room.

Toni turned to Danny. "A copy?" she said. "Wow! I didn't see that coming. You really think Kate doesn't know about this?"

Danny shook his head. "*You* saw her. She *seems* genuinely worried. I think she's scared to death that she's about to lose her dad's painting—the real one. If it's a fake, I'll bet it's a surprise to her. She might have just gotten lucky, and she doesn't even know it."

Toni stared at the print of the painting. After a few seconds, she said, "Don't start celebrating just yet. If it's *not* real, Kate might have just gotten *unlucky*. This is *not* good news. Think about it: If they even consider selling it, or taking it to the auction—"

"Oh, crap! You're right!" he said. "If they try to sell it, then sooner or later, someone's going to check it out." He took a quick breath. "If the Thornes find out that they paid a half million dollars for what they think is a two-million-dollar painting, but then they find out that it's actually a fake, they're gonna want payback all right. But it's gonna be an entirely different kind of payback."

* * * *

"There!" Toni said, pointing. "That alleyway over there—Sylvia said it's a light green building." They were a mile south of the Mariners baseball stadium in the Sodo district, home to an eclectic mix of buildings, some practically new, others built in the 1890s and waiting their turn at regentrification. Near the back of a tight little entranceway was a single door.

Danny pointed to a plywood sign above the door with 3010 painted on it in faded red letters. "This is us."

Toni looked around as they walked over, a scowl on her face. "First-class joint."

Inside, they found a hallway lit by yellowing fluorescent lights that buzzed and flickered on, then off, then on again. The wall directory had white letters pressed into a faded black corrugated background. One line read "Wm. Hol ins: 319"—the second l in Hollins having fallen off at some point.

The elevator was located just past the directory. Danny pushed the button, and the doors rolled open, creaking in protest. A smell wafted their way, a sour blend of cigarette smoke, mold, and urine. Toni wrinkled her nose, then moved to cover her mouth with a sleeve. She took a step back and shook her head.

"No way," she said. "Imagine getting stuck in that thing. I'd kill myself." She looked to her left, then nodded that direction. "Stairs." She turned and marched off down the hall, Danny following behind.

On the third floor, things were much the same—same faded linoleum floors, same dim, flickering lighting as the first floor, slightly less offensive smell. They walked down the hall, and Danny located a red and white hand-lettered sign that read "319—Wm. Hollins" taped to a door. He tried the handle, but it was locked. He gave a sharp knock.

At first, there was no sound, but a moment later, they heard the faint shuffling of someone inside moving about. Danny tapped Toni on the shoulder, and when she looked at him, he made a "spread out" motion. Toni nodded and moved from the center of the door to a position on the right side while he did the same on the left. He knocked again. This time, after a couple of seconds, the door suddenly jerked partially open, and the long chrome barrel of a very large .44 Magnum revolver popped out.

Danny's eyes opened wide. His right hand shot forward and grabbed the barrel of the gun, pulling it straight out toward the hallway and pushing upward. At the same time, he reached over with his left hand and yanked on the door handle, closing it hard on the wrist of the hand that held the weapon.

"Ow!" the man inside cried, immediately opening his hand and releasing the pistol.

A split second later, Danny had the revolver in hand and flipped it around. He shoved hard on the door, knocking the surprised little man inside backward, flat on his back. Danny stood in the doorway and pointed the gun down at him.

The man was in his early sixties, short, very thin, and bald with a dark mustache. He raised trembling hands, his eyes wide. "No! No! Don't shoot me! Don't shoot!"

Danny glared at him for a moment. "Do you always answer your door like that?" Before the man could answer, Danny asked, "Are you Will Hollins?"

The man glanced at Toni, then back at Danny. "Who are you? What are you doing outside my door?" He sat up and rubbed his forearm. "You almost broke my wrist!"

"You're lucky I didn't. I'm Danny Logan, and this is Toni Blair. Sylvia Lyon sent us. She called while we were on the way. Didn't you talk to her?"

He shook his head. "Sylvia? No, she didn't. I didn't talk to anybody. Did she call? I turn my phone off when I'm working so I don't get disturbed."

Danny looked up and down the hall, then back at the small man. "May we come in?"

Will nodded toward the gun, eyeing Danny warily. "You're the one with the gun."

"Which I will return to you in a minute if you promise to behave yourself." He lowered the gun. "Now put your hands down and get up. We're not here to hurt you."

"Then why . . ."

"We just wanted to ask you some questions. Geez." They

entered as Will got to his feet.

"Why'd you answer the door like that?" Danny said.

"Bad neighbors," Will said, relief returning to his voice. He nodded toward the door. "Better lock it."

The heavy metal door had four deadbolts. Danny locked them all, then turned back to Will.

"Before we go any further, let's clear things up and put your mind at ease. Why don't you go ahead and get Sylvia on the phone so she can verify who we are? Then I don't have to worry about you pulling a hidey gun from somewhere and shooting us."

* * * *

Two minutes later, Will hung up the phone and turned to Danny. "I'm sorry for the misunderstanding. Can't be too careful, you know?"

"So we're good, then?" Danny said.

"Yeah. Sylvia told me what's going on. Pays to be cautious. That painting over there is worth over four million bucks."

Danny looked toward the far wall. The entire side of the large studio space was paneled in smooth varnished plywood that stretched from floor to ceiling and made a huge vertical work surface. Paintings were mounted at intervals along the wall. Will pointed to an elaborate array of photographic lights with umbrellas pointed toward a colorful painting hung in the center of the wall. Next to the lights, a high-tech-looking camera was aimed at the painting.

"That one there in the middle?" Danny asked. "Four million bucks? Wow."

"Yeah, I don't like to keep them here for long. Makes me nervous."

"So we noticed."

"I keep 'em just long enough for me to shoot photos. Then I send them home. Matter of fact, I usually like the owner or the owner's rep to stay while I shoot 'em. The rep for the guy that owns that one was just here, but he had to run off for an hour. He left a few minutes ago, so when I heard you outside, I knew it wasn't him at the door. I was worried."

"You'd never guess looking from the outside that that kind of thing would be in here," Toni said, staring at the painting.

Will smiled. "I know, right?" He leaned forward. "I'm incognito. It's one of the few advantages of operating out of a dump like this."

"Cheap rent's probably another," Danny mused.

"Yeah," Will said. He leaned back and looked around. "Of course, there are disadvantages, too. As you probably saw, the décor outside's a little rough, and we have more than our share of desperados running around outside. I'd say someone finds their way up here and tries to break in maybe twice a month or so, looking for dope money, I suppose. Lucky for me, that kinda stuff seems random, and they're unsophisticated. No one's ever made it through my steel door. But I gotta be careful, especially when I have a painting here. When I'm working and I hear someone fiddling with the door handle, I just naturally assume the worst."

Danny nodded. "Thus the hand cannon." He popped open

the revolver's cylinder and unloaded the giant cartridges into his hand, then he handed Will back his pistol and the cartridges. "Reload it after we leave. You're safe enough for now."

"Thanks. Sylvia said you guys had some questions," he said as he set the gun on a nearby table. "You want to sit down? I owe Sylvia a bunch of favors, so I'm all yours."

After they were seated, Danny pulled out his phone and showed Will the photo of *Lilies* that Sylvia had emailed them. "You ever see this painting before?"

Will slipped on a pair of reading glasses and leaned forward, then he smiled. "Yeah, sure. This is Taylor Morgan's Sisley."

"Did you make a copy of it for him?"

"Sure did. Couple of years ago, right after he bought it."

Danny glanced over at Toni. "Sylvia was right."

She nodded. "Do you know where Taylor Morgan keeps the original?" Toni asked.

"Yeah, I think he keeps most of his collection—the good stuff—at Friars in New York—Friars Fine Art Storage. Their couriers always wait for it while I do the photos. It's like they're guarding the president. Soon as I'm done, they're out of here."

Toni asked, "How good is your copy?"

"How *good* is it? What do you mean? It's excellent, of course. It's basically a photocopy."

"A photocopy?"

Will smiled. "I don't paint 'em from scratch. What I do is I make a fancy digital print called a giclée. I take a super-high-quality photo of the original—just like I'm doing with that one on the wall over there. Then, after the photos, I make an ultrahigh-resolution color print, usually on canvas. I stretch the canvas on a frame that I've made on the table here, treat it with a UV spray, then I do what's known as embellishing. Which is a fancy way of saying that I add about fifty thousand brushstrokes over the top of the print to enhance the texture on the canvas. It's a technique that I've worked out. When they're dry, my 'embellishments' blend right in with the print underneath. Gives it the feel of canvas with real brushstrokes, almost just like the original."

"And you can't tell the difference from the original?" Toni asked.

"Well, *I* can tell. But most lay people can't. Come look for yourself." He popped up, and the two followed him. "See this one?"

They looked closely at an oil painting on the wall.

"I'm about halfway done with it."

Danny leaned closer. "That's not a painting?"

Will smiled. "Nope."

"Wow," Toni said. "I'd have never guessed. The brushstrokes, the canvas, it looks totally real."

"Go ahead and touch it. It's dry."

They each ran their fingertips lightly across the canvas. "Feels just like brushstrokes," Danny said.

"That's because they *are* brushstrokes. *My* brushes, *my* strokes. I study the masters, their techniques. I'm pretty good at following them."

"Amazing." Danny stared for a second. "You really can't tell. Which leads to another question. Not counting last night, I'd never even seen a giclée—"

"As far as you know," Will said.

Danny nodded. "True. What I'm saying is, obviously you can fool me pretty easy—I don't know diddly about it. But the question is, say you got someone who was going to buy what they thought was an original painting. Would they be able to tell the difference?"

Will shrugged. "Depends on how sophisticated and how smart they are. Smart buyers hire someone who knows what they're doing to check it out–especially when you get up into the *Lilies* price range. Then again, in this business, a lot of people have more money than smarts and they sometimes fly by the seat of their pants. One of my prints could easily fool someone who don't know what to look for."

"But if the buyer *was* smart enough to bring in an art expert to check it out?" Toni asked. "Could the reproduction fool an art expert?"

"Again, it depends. Depends on the expert—their experience and expertise. To be safe, I'd say no, it wouldn't fool a legitimate expert. Then again, lots of people call themselves art experts in this business, and they can't tell a pastel from a Crayola. Those people get fooled all the time. Bear in mind, I don't make copies to fool the experts—that's not the point of what I do."

"Understood," Danny said. "Say one of your copies went to a major auction house, like Christie's, would they routinely check out a painting before they put it up for auction?"

"Christie's?" He chuckled. "Yeah, definitely. They don't want any scandals damaging their reputation."

"And they'd be able to spot a reproduction?"

"Oh, hell yeah. They're pros. They've got *real* experts. That's one of the things they look for, and they're good at it. It'd take them all of about thirty seconds to sniff out a reproduction. Maybe less."

"Even if it was a reproduction as good as yours?"

"If you took this to Christie's for an auction, they'd laugh you right out of the place, if they didn't have you arrested first."

Danny stared at him, then nodded slowly. "Good to know. I—" His phone buzzed. He glanced at the text message, then handed the phone to Toni. "It's from Kate."

Billy Thorne just left. Said someone tried to steal the painting last night. Acts like he thinks it was me. I told him to piss off.

"Thanks for your help, Will," Danny said, standing. "We've got what we need."

They started to leave, but Danny turned back. "Do yourself a favor. Spend fifty bucks and buy a doorbell camera."

CHAPTER 5

Desperate Measures

Next morning, a small group of colorful one-man Laser-class sailboats beat to the windward mark in a gentle breeze on Lake Union. Several hundred yards away, a white and yellow Kenmore Air Otter seaplane swung wide around the racers as it taxied into take-off position at the far south end of the lake. Danny watched the activity through the Logan Private Investigations conference room windows before he turned and glanced at the clock on the wall. It was two minutes before nine.

Toni was already seated at the table, next to a tall, distinguished-looking man with silver hair. The two were huddled together, laughing quietly.

"What's so funny?" Danny asked as he slid into his normal seat at the head of the table.

Toni smiled. "I was telling Richard how I almost flipped you right out of the boat when I gunned it."

Danny chuckled. "Wasn't very funny at the time. Good thing I grabbed hold."

"She did well, though?" Richard asked.

"Yeah—aside from almost dumping me into the lake, yeah, she did great. Drove it like a Navy SEAL. Doc taught her well. Speaking of which, where is he? And Kenny, too?"

"We're here." A short, slender, dark-haired young man rushed into the conference room.

"Good morning, Kenny," Toni said cheerily.

"Yo."

Kenny was followed by another man—tall, muscular, graceful of movement. His sharp facial features were deeply tanned and his shiny black hair was tied back in a short ponytail. The man nodded to Danny. "Boss."

"Morning, Doc."

Kenny reached across the table and handed a remote-control device to Richard as he and Doc took their seats. "This should do ya. It just needed batteries."

"Let's get started," Danny said. He turned to Richard. "You're up."

Richard shifted back in his seat. "Thank you, sir." He turned to a large video screen mounted on the wall at the far end of the table and pointed the remote. "After we talked yesterday afternoon, I started . . ." A photo of Frank Thorne filled the screen. "Ah, *there* he is. Meet Frank Thorne, Seattle's most notorious hard-money lender and occasional loan shark."

They studied the photo as Richard continued. "I gave a call to a couple of the SPD old-timers that I trained—guys still active. They filled me in on the details. Thorne's in what you might call the high-risk-loan business. He focuses on lending money to people who shouldn't be borrowing in the first place, then he takes advantage of them when they can't pay him back."

"Sounds like a funny business model," Kenny said, "lending to people who can't repay. A good way to go broke."

"You might think, until you understand that the people Thorne makes loans to are usually so desperate for money that he's able to demand crazy-high interest plus oversized collateral when he makes the loan. My guys said his MO is to walk in with a huge bag of cash and toss it on the table. People's eyes light up, and they're so desperate, they have a hard time turning him down. Too bad, because he loads up the deal in his favor. If he gets paid back, that's okay—he collects a massive amount of interest. And if he doesn't get paid back, that's okay, too, because he just sits back and keeps the collateral. Sells it later for a big profit. Boats, cars, real estate . . . artwork. He's actually turned *that* angle into an art form. The man's been playing this game for a long time, and he's good at it."

"Sounds just like Kate's deal," Toni said.

"Agreed," Richard said. "Vintage Frank Thorne. Of course, with the added little wrinkle this time that he apparently hasn't figured out yet that the collateral he's holding is essentially worthless." He pressed the remote.

"These next pictures are from yesterday afternoon on Kate's movie set. As you know, while you were down in Sodo visiting the art dealer, she had visitors. She saw these three guys walking up, and she managed to grab a few cell phone photos before she went outside and confronted them."

"First question—how'd they get through the police line?" Toni asked. "When we were there, we got stopped. There were at least three or four SPD officers running security."

"I asked her that very question and it turns out that they had legit set passes. Kate said she confronted her partner about it, and he admitted giving 'em the passes a couple of weeks ago."

"That was nice of him," Toni said, shaking her head.

Richard turned to the screen. "Anyways, the young, dark-haired guy here in front is *Billy* Thorne—Frank's only child, from his first marriage. The consensus is that young Billy's the gangster-equivalent of a trust-fund baby. I'm told he mostly chases drugs, booze, and expensive women. Frank doesn't seem to care, as long as Billy stays in the background and keeps out of any kind of big trouble."

"Which is a little confusing, then," Danny said, "seeing's how Billy seems to be running point on this deal with Kate."

"This is true. I suppose it's possible that Billy is trying to expand into daddy's business, maybe make his bones on this deal." He shrugged. "But I've gotta believe that with a half-million-dollar loan and a two-million-dollar painting as collateral, Frank's got him on a pretty short leash."

He pointed to the bald man standing behind Billy Thorne. "This guy here in the soccer jersey we couldn't ID. The boys at SPD are still looking into him for me. Kate said he rarely talks—acts like a bodyguard, which is probably exactly what he is—Billy Thorne's bodyguard."

Toni pointed to the third man. "Who's the little guy? Were

you able to ID him?"

Richard smiled and zoomed in. "The little guy—yeah, that one's easy. That's Farley Palmer."

"*That's* Farley Palmer?" Danny asked, leaning forward.

"Who's Farley Palmer?" Kenny asked.

"He's a PI," Danny said. "The competition."

"Actually," Richard said, "like myself, Palmer's a former lieutenant in the Seattle Police Department detective bureau. And yes, he *is* a PI, but not in your guy's league, though. I think he has a small, one-man shop. Keeps an office over in Belltown somewhere."

Danny glanced at Richard. "You know him?"

"I do," Richard said. "Farley and I were partners for a stretch. We were teamed up in the late eighties, up till the year before I retired and started the agency here. I worked with him for about five years." He stared at the photo for a moment.

"Farley's an excellent detective—gifted, even. He comes across as very low-key—he's got this Columbo shtick down cold." He stopped, noticing the blank looks on the faces of the others. "You know Columbo, right? Peter Falk? 'Excuse me, ma'am . . .' No?" He shook his head. "Geez, it's no fun getting old. Anyway, Farley's a very smart guy. His method was all about flying under the radar. He snooped about so unobtrusively, you hardly noticed he was there. Never pushy, never stood out, never yelled. No one saw him coming. But he was relentless. He went along all quiet like, putting his case together—A, followed by B, followed by C, then, when he was ready, BAM! He had you."

"What's he doing working for a man like Frank Thorne?"

Danny asked.

Richard shook his head. "Good question, and one for which I have no answer. I know he used to hate the Frank Thorne types. Why that seems to have changed, I don't know. I haven't spoken to Farley in a long time. His wife passed away several years ago, and Farley didn't take it well. I remember he used to always talk about how he was going to retire so they could move to a beach house in Mexico. After she died, though, he sort of just . . . deflated. He ended up taking early retirement from SPD—dropped out of sight. I ran into him a couple of years later, and he seemed sort of okay, but we never really connected." He stared at the photo. "I have no idea why he'd want to associate with Frank Thorne."

"Well, he looks like a professor. He doesn't look mean enough to be an old-time cop," Kenny said.

Richard chuckled. "Looks can be deceiving, young man. You're right—Farley was never what you'd call a badass—not physically, anyways. I mean, he was a decent shot, used to carry a tiny little .38 revolver. But his favorite toy—he used to carry this black leather sap, a little strap of thick hard leather about six, eight inches long, couple inches wide. It had a piece of lead sewn into the end. You wouldn't see him coming and he'd give a quick smack on the arm with that thing. The perp would go numb for thirty minutes. Better than a Taser. If he was really annoyed with someone, he'd just give 'em a little tap upside the head, and they'd be out cold for ten minutes or so."

"What you'd call the direct approach," Kenny said.

Richard nodded. "You bet. Of course, SPD outlawed saps

some time ago, got tired of defending the lawsuits, I suppose, but it was my generation's version of nonlethal force. Better to get your lights turned out temporarily with a sap than permanently with a bullet." He looked at Danny. "Like I said, it's been years since I had any contact, but Farley was a good detective. If he's working for Frank Thorne, and"—he glanced at the screen—"it appears that he is, we'll have to pay special attention."

"Thanks," Danny said. He turned to the group. "Well? You guys know what's happened over the past couple of days. You know about Kate's predicament. Now you've got a little background on the Thornes. What do you think?"

Toni shrugged. "What can we do? So far, it's just been threats and talk. The loan's technically not due for another four or five weeks. Seems like there's nothing we can do but wait and let Kate come up with the money to pay back the loan."

"Normally, I'd agree," Richard said. "But in this case, waiting could well be quite dangerous. You'd be relying on the *hope* that the Thornes don't discover the painting they're holding is a fake while Kate waits to get her post-production loan together. This might not be wise, especially when we suspect that the Thornes apparently want to keep the painting, probably to sell it for a profit. If that happens, any *real* buyer's going to want to authenticate it before they fork over the cash. In my opinion, the odds of Thorne discovering the fake before the September 16 due date are high. That will be bad news, indeed."

"You might be right," she said, "but again, the Thornes haven't done anything illegal so far. There's nothing we can do, at least now. I don't want us to step in and do something stupid and we end up being the only ones guilty of anything."

"Good point," Richard said, nodding.

The room was quiet for a minute, the picture of Billy Thorne at the movie set staring down at the team. Finally, Danny shook his head. "This sucks. Toni's right that the Thornes technically haven't done anything wrong . . . yet. So we can't step in . . . yet. But Richard's right, too. If you think someone's out to kill you, it might be best to not just sit around and wait to find out if you're right."

Danny mulled it over. "We can't just sit on our butts and wait for the hammer to fall. We have to come up with something so we can force the issue, flush the Thornes out before they figure things out on their own." He glanced at Toni. "All without putting ourselves in legal jeopardy."

"You got some sort of bright idea?" Toni asked.

Danny smiled. "I'm working on it."

Toni tilted her head and gave him a stern look.

It was quiet for several seconds, then Richard leaned forward. "I've got an idea. What if the Thornes could be persuaded to just give the painting up?"

Danny looked at him. "What? Ask them to just hand it over?"

"Yes. Voluntarily. Forget all about trying to sell it. No sale, no checking it out, no chance of discovery that it's a copy."

"Why would they do that?" Doc asked, a skeptical look on his face. "The Thornes don't seem like magnanimous types."

Richard chuckled. "No, they don't. But what if they had a proper inducement, something to make them care less about the painting and more about another . . . bigger opportunity?"

Danny tilted his head. "You mean like make 'em an offer they can't refuse?"

"Something like that. A better offer—something that appeals to them."

Danny motioned with his hand. "Go on."

Richard took a deep breath, then let it out slowly. "I can't believe I'm about to suggest this, but I might have an idea that falls squarely into the category of 'desperate times call for desperate measures.' Any of you ever hear the name Henry Parker?"

"Nope," Danny said. He glanced at Toni.

"Me neither."

Doc and Kenny both shook their heads.

Richard continued. "Not surprising, I suppose. Henry Parker is the single greatest living practitioner of the long con in America today. He's really good at it. So good, in fact, that outside of law enforcement, hardly anyone's ever seen him or even heard of him."

"Long con? He's a confidence artist?" Danny asked. "A con man?"

"Not just your average, everyday rip-off artist con man," Richard said. "Henry's the acknowledged master of the *long* con. He might have some ideas that could help us."

Toni furrowed her brow and gave him a hard look. "Wait a second. I'm not sure I'm believing what I'm hearing. The guy's a con artist you say? Are you seriously about to suggest that we somehow get involved with a man like that? I just finished saying I don't want us to do anything illegal, and now you're suggesting we team up with a con artist? Come on, Richard. We're already guilty of sneaking on to a man's property in the middle of the night and peeping through his window." She shook her head. "I can't believe I went along with that. But we got lucky. Don't forget, Danny got shot at, for crying out loud."

Richard nodded. "I admit, it's unusual. But I think what we may have here is an interesting philosophical question. If you commit a little crime in order to prevent a big crime, did you really commit a crime at all? Or is the little one somehow canceled out?" He paused. "Is it something you'd consider?"

Danny shrugged. "Normally? I don't want us to commit *any* crimes–big or little. But . . . if it's the only answer, and if it meant Kate and Ray don't have to face retribution from Frank Thorne, I'd say we'd have to at least consider it."

Toni shook her head. "Not me. Don't get me wrong–I feel bad that your friend's in a tight spot. And I hear what you and Richard are saying, but I don't want to even consider something like what you guys are talking about unless we had rock solid proof that the Thorne's actually did something wrong, or at least were about to. Not just threats, either. Real, tangible proof."

Silence filled the room. Seconds ticked by. Finally, Kenny said, "Say we *could* figure out a way to get clear. How do we even know we can get a hold of this Henry Parker fellow in time to do something?"

"If I'm not mistaken," Richard said, "I think this case has . . . features . . . that might appeal to Henry."

Danny narrowed his eyes. "You sound like you know him."

"I know him because I arrested him," Richard added. "Many years ago. Twice, actually."

Danny tilted his head. "You busted him twice, and you still think he's the best in the land?"

Richard smiled. "Meaning, how can he be the best in the land if he's been busted, especially by little ol' me?"

"Sorry–meant no offense."

"None taken. Besides, you needn't worry. Henry beat the rap. Both times."

It was quiet for a few seconds, then Toni shrugged. She turned to Danny. "I guess the ball's in your court. You know how I feel. Before we move, you gotta come up with something to make Thorne show his cards."

Danny smiled. "I think an idea just came to me that'll tell us exactly where the Thornes are coming from. I need to get Kate on board, but I think she'll see it."

* * * *

"That's nuts!" Kate's eyes widened as a look of alarm came over her face. "I can't call Billy Thorne and tell him I have the money to pay him off next week, because I don't. It's impossible. This is your plan? It's crazy."

Danny and Toni were seated across from her at a table near the front window of Duke's Chowder House on Lake Union. The dinner crowd had not quite kicked in yet, and the restaurant was still relatively quiet.

Kate leaned forward. "Yesterday," she said, her voice lowered, "you guys said that he has to give us the time he and Ray agreed on. Which means I still have a month before the loan's due." She looked at Toni, then back to Danny. "A whole month. You're forcing things too early."

Danny shook his head. "Yesterday we didn't know what we know now. And believe me, we're not forcing anything."

"You have Ray to thank for that," Toni said, "when he stole that painting—."

"And the painting turned out to be a copy," Danny added.

Toni nodded. "Right. When he did that, Ray put your lives in danger. If the Thornes figure out it's a fake, they're gonna' come after you, both of you. You could *die*, you understand?"

"Kate," Danny said, "clock's ticking. The Thornes don't have to give you thirty days or even thirty minutes. I think it's only because Billy Thorne must be a real knucklehead that they haven't figured it out yet. But that won't last. It could turn around *any* time, *especially* if they're going to try and keep the painting and sell it. For all we know, they could walk through that door right now."

"*That's* why we're pressing," Toni said.

Kate glanced at the door, then she turned and stared out the window at the boats pulling out of the marina, a grim look on her face.

"Kate," Danny said, "listen to me. You've got a brief window of tactical advantage to get this thing back under control. You know the painting's a copy—they don't. You've got the upper hand. Use it."

"How do we know they don't already know it's a fake?" Kate asked, turning to him.

"How do–?" Danny smiled. "I don't think there'll be much confusion if the Thornes figure it out. I mean, I don't take them to be overly subtle."

Kate gave him a hard look. "Yeah . . . well, if I offer to pay them back early, what happens if they say, 'Yeah, go ahead'? Where do I get the cash? Who's got that kind of money?"

Danny raised an eyebrow and tilted his head, staring back. A second later, her eyes opened wide. "Oh my God! I can't believe I didn't see it. If they say yes, you guys want me to call my father for the money. That's your fallback? I already told you guys why that's a serious problem for me."

"You did," Danny said. "But, again, this is in the context of we know more now than we did yesterday. Yesterday, we thought the downside was you lose the painting. Today, we know that the downside is that you lose your life. Big difference."

Kate said nothing, simply stared at Danny.

"But remember," Danny continued. "It's only in the very slim off-chance that the Thornes are willing to accept payment that you'd have to face your dad. I really don't think it's going to come to that. I still think your original concern is right—it's a lot more likely when you offer to pay off the loan early, they're going to come up with some bullshit excuse and basically tell you to take a hike. They won't let you pay it off because they want the painting."

"So why do it, then?" Kate asked. "Why go through the exercise? They already threatened to sell it. In fact, they said they already had a buyer. That's not good enough proof of what they want to do?"

Danny shook his head. "Nah, they talked about it, but we don't know they've actually sold it. We *do* know that—for now, anyway—they still have it. For all we know, the threats might be nothing more than Billy Thorne's heavy-handed way of putting pressure on you to make sure you pay them back. It's not enough for us to take action on. That's why we want to call their bluff."

"Believe me, Kate," Toni said, "I was skeptical at first. But Danny came up with this idea to flush out the Thornes, and I think it makes sense. It may be the only way to get them to turn over their cards and show us what they really mean to do. We have to know for certain before we can step in."

Kate turned and stared out the window across Lake Union. When she turned back, tears had formed in her eyes. "It gets better and better," she said. "I don't know what's worse—facing the Thornes if they say no, or facing my father if they say yes."

"I'm sorry about all this," Danny said. "Is Ray any help at all to you?"

Kate took a quick breath. "Short answer? No, Ray's no help. In fact, he keeps making things worse." She took a deep breath. "Things are to the point that I don't even know where he is half the time."

Danny glanced at Toni, then turned back to Kate. "I'm sorry about that, too, then," he said. "I wish you weren't having to go through any of this.'"

Kate pursed her lips. Then she nodded. "Me, too, but I guess I am. If you think that this is what it takes to make it happen, then yeah, set it up."

* * * *

Frank Thorne's office door was open when Billy walked in without knocking. Doyle was seated across from Thorne, the two men wrapped up in a conversation. They stopped and looked at Billy.

"You guys won't believe the phone call I just got."

Frank looked up, and several seconds ticked by as he waited, Billy milking the scene for all the drama he could. Finally, his patience dried up. "Yeah, well, you going to tell us, or we gotta guess?"

"Right." Billy pulled up a chair and sat down. "Kate Morgan called. She wants to have a meeting tomorrow. She says her new loan just came through, and she has the money to pay us off."

"What?" Frank sat up straight in his chair. "Today she said that? I thought you said they needed to finish filming in order to get a loan. Are they done?"

"That's what they been saying. And far as I know, they aren't done. Not as of yesterday, anyway. But that's what she said. She says she wants to have a meeting tomorrow and pay us off next Tuesday, so she must have got a line on the cash from somewhere."

Frank stared at him, an intense, penetrating stare. He took a deep breath and shook his head. "What a day this is turning out to be." He leaned back, his eyes focusing on a spot on the wall over Billy's head. Then he turned to Doyle. "When's that loan due again?"

Doyle punched a few commands into his phone. "The sixteenth, boss. September the sixteenth."

"And when's that auction at Christie's?"

"It's on . . ." He looked it up. "It's on September 9—week before the due date."

"Which makes it, what? A little over four weeks from now?"

"Yeah. Exactly."

"And the next one after that?"

"What? The next big auction?"

"Yeah, the next big auction. What do you think I'm talking about?"

"The next really big one's not for another six months."

"Six months." Frank leaned back and rubbed his chin for a moment, then he suddenly stood up. "The auction's four weeks away. That's four weeks from us turning a five-hundred-thousand-dollar investment into a two-million-dollar payday. That's something I don't want us to miss out on. But now this woman wants to just pay us off and thinks we should be happy with a hundred-thousand-dollar vig instead?" He turned to Billy. "What do you say? This is *your* deal. Are you okay with that?"

Billy looked at him for a moment, then shook his head. "No, Pop, of course not. But we have an agreement. If she has the money, how do we . . ."

"To hell with the agreement!" Thorne yelled, slamming his hand on the desk. His face reddened. "The woman's out of her friggin' mind. We ain't in business to make a teeny bit of interest, got it? We're not gonna get this close to the payoff, then get the door slammed in our faces." He put his hands on the desk. "You two listen to me. That woman ain't gettin' that painting back, and that's that." It was quiet for a couple of seconds. Frank stared at each of them, first one, then the other.

Neither man appeared anxious to speak, but finally Billy said, "I agree one hundred percent, Pop. She can't pay us off, no way. That's nuts. But . . . but how do we hold her off? Doesn't she have the legal right to pay the loan off?"

Frank laughed. "Legal right? Legal right, my ass." He turned to Doyle. "It's time for Article 14."

Doyle nodded, "Article 14."

Billy furrowed his brow. "What's Article 14?"

Frank gave him a hard look. "Article 14? If you spent more time around here without the coke spoon up your nose, you'd already know. Doyle, tell him what Article 14 is."

"It's the 'anything else' clause, sort of what you'd call a catch-all. It's built into the paperwork on all our loans. It basically means I call the lawyer and tell him to make something up."

Frank gave a quick nod. "Exactly. And I don't care what it is. Call Peter Hayes. He'll come up with something. He's good at coming up with crap like this. But whatever it is, keep this in mind—the woman does not get that painting back! Got it?"

"Got it, Pop."

Frank turned to Doyle. "And you, you get Ernie and Theo to pay a little visit to that movie set tonight. Whoever that woman's getting her funds from, I want 'em to start having second thoughts, like maybe that film *ain't* gonna finish on time after all. I want that thing slowed down. Things are starting to get out of hand here." He turned to Billy. "You better get in control of this thing, Bill. You got it?"

Billy nodded. "I do. I'm on it."

CHAPTER 6
Assault

Toni handed Danny a mug full of Mac & Jack's African Amber ale. It was eleven p.m., and Danny was stretched out on a lounger on their patio, relaxing after a long day, watching the late-night summer boat traffic on Lake Union.

"Thanks."

"Sure." She slid into the lounger beside Danny. "So, I hear Kate saved your butt in Iraq."

He turned to her. "Yeah? Where'd you hear that?"

"From Doc."

He turned back, chuckling. "Doc? Doc wasn't nowhere near. He was in a whole different province up in the mountains somewhere with the rest of the snake-eaters doing their Special Forces thing. Hell, I didn't even meet him until I got to Fort Lewis."

"I know. But he knows the story. He says everyone who was in Iraq at the time heard about it."

Danny grimaced and shook his head. "I doubt it."

"That's what he says. Care to set the record straight?"

Danny stared at the lights reflecting on the lake. He shrugged, then said, "Okay. One night, we were making a quick snatch-and-grab in some little craphole of a village in western Iraq. Supposed to arrest this dude that someone thought was a high-value hajji. So we came around a corner after midnight, and bam! Our lead vehicle gets hit by an IED. It was bad. Flames. Screamin'. Injured guys piling out. We were a convoy of three vehicles. I was in the tail vehicle, and we couldn't move. Almost immediately, we started taking fire. It was chaos. Fortunately, we happened to luck out and have two medics with us that night. They started in taking care of the wounded, everyone else returning fire, trying to keep 'em off us. But they had us boxed in good and tight. A couple minutes later, they opened up with RPGs, and boom! Both of the other vehicles got hit, and that was that. We were pinned down behind a wall, surrounded and in deep shit, with wounded men and no way out."

"You must have been terrified."

Danny nodded. "Probably a little. But we were busy. Things were happening fast, and we were just sort of reacting, trying to get organized." He paused. "It was definitely intense, that's for sure. Then our lieutenant got hit in the shoulder so now I'm in charge. I managed to get everybody hunkered down in the best defensive position we could manage, and we returned fire, held 'em off for the moment, but we were taking a lot of rounds. We were in trouble. We radioed for help, and they told us to hold tight for fifteen minutes. Fifteen friggin' minutes! I told 'em I wasn't sure we could do that."

Danny took a pull from his beer. "It was pretty sketchy there for a bit. All of a sudden—I don't know, maybe five, seven minutes later, something like that—this deuce and a half comes flying around a corner between two buildings from a direction that was relatively quiet. The bad guys hadn't figured anyone would try to come in that way, so they weren't covering it. The truck comes roaring up to us and skids to a stop in a big ol' cloud of dust. They're taking fire like crazy, but out pops this kid truck driver—PFC Kate Morgan. I'll never forget—she yells out, 'Somebody call for a cab?' I couldn't believe it. First thing I told her is to get her silly ass down before she got smoked. Then we proceeded to load up our wounded, half of us laying down cover fire, the other half loading the injured, getting shot at the whole time. A friggin' miracle no one else got hit. Took just a couple of minutes, but once we were all loaded up, Kate hopped back in and hauled ass backward. Backed out the same way she came in. Drove that sucker in reverse until we were in the clear. She told me she was part of the end of a convoy nearby when she heard our radio call. She'd peeled off the back and scooted on over. Just like that. Saved our asses. Aside from our lieutenant, and the wounded guys when the Humvees went up, the only other casualty was Kate's shotgun rider. Took a tiny piece of shrapnel in the arm on the way out. No one died."

Toni stared at him for a moment. "Wow. That's quite a story."

"Yeah . . . that's how it happened." He took a pull from his beer, then set it down. "Funny thing—maybe not so funny—is Kate actually got in trouble for peeling off from her convoy and coming to help without permission. That's the official reason, anyway. We all thought that the real reason the brass was pissed was that they had just spent a year or two running around telling everyone that women weren't in combat, and then along comes Kate, a teenage girl who runs right into the middle of a combat zone. They didn't know how to handle it. In the end, they didn't have much of a choice because her old man's connected and she had too many people speaking up for her. So the brass switched gears, said she wasn't actually a combatant *in* combat, she was a noncombatant who happened to be *near* combat." He shrugged. "Whatever. They ended up giving her a Silver Star. Okay by me. Seeing's how I might not be here if it weren't for her, I'd say she damn sure earned it."

Toni took a deep breath and stared at him for a moment. "There's still a lot about you I don't know, you know?"

He laughed. "Yeah, right. That's not true. You know about all the big things."

Toni shook her head. "I thought so, but just when I think that's the case, along comes another little nugget like this. No wonder you feel obligated to help her."

"S'pose so."

"Was there anything else between the two of you?"

He turned to her. "Anything else? You mean like . . .?"

"You know what I mean—anything else. I mean, if there was, I'm cool with it. It was pre-me, right? And Kate's an impressive woman—smart, good-looking, war hero, her old man owns half of friggin' Bellevue. She's hot—I get it. I just want to know. If there was something between the two of you, I don't want to be the only one around here who doesn't know about it."

Danny smiled. "Fair enough. Here's the deal. I was, like, twenty-one at the time. Kate was, I think, barely a year out of high school. We were both from Seattle. We happened to be stuck in a crappy place at the same time doing a crappy job. We became friends. We were in different units, but I bumped into her from time to time."

"And?"

"And?" He smiled. "There is no *and*. We were just friends for about a year before I got sent home. There was never anything else. Just friends. And for the record, she's got nothing on you."

Toni took a deep breath and let it out slowly. "Thanks. So where's that leave us?"

He glanced at her. "What do you mean?"

"The case."

"Oh—that. I guess it's hard for me to get past the fact that I basically owe Kate my life. She was there when I needed help. Now she needs my help, so the way I see it, I gotta do what I can to be there for her."

Toni nodded. "I get it. Do you really think your plan's going to work. Do you think the Thornes are going to show their cards tomorrow?"

He smiled. "I do. We poked 'em pretty good today. I'll bet when Kate meets with 'em tomorrow—" Danny stopped and stared at the skyline to the southwest, in the direction of the Space Needle. "Something's on fire. See that smoke over there?"

Toni turned. "Yeah. It looks like it's—"

Danny's phone rang and cut her off. He looked at the number, then glanced at Toni. "Kate."

"Kate?" he answered. "What's goin' on?" A few seconds later, he sat up and said, "Okay. We're on our way."

He hung up and turned to Toni. "The movie set's on fire."

* * * *

Danny and Toni hopped out of the Jeep and hurried over to the area cordoned off with yellow POLICE LINE DO NOT CROSS tape just as a Seattle police officer moved a barrier to allow an ambulance to pull away from the movie set.

"Uh-oh," Toni said. "Someone got hurt." She covered her ears as the ambulance kicked its siren on and roared away. At the far side of the set, opposite Kate's motor home, a team of firefighters was hosing off a raging vehicle fire.

"Keep back!" a policeman yelled to Danny as they approached the barricade.

"It's okay!" Danny turned and saw Kate running over. "They're with me!" she said.

When she reached them, he grabbed Kate by the shoulders. "You all right?"

She nodded, smoke streaks on her face. "Yeah." She sniffed. "Son of a bitch!"

"What happened?" Toni asked.

Kate turned and pointed to the vehicle fire. "Little while ago, maybe a little before eleven—I was in the office working on bills—I hear Eddie yelling, 'Fire!'"

"Eddie G?"

Kate nodded. "Yeah. I grabbed my cell phone and ran outside." She pointed. "That car over there was on fire, big-time. It's mostly out now, but when we first saw it, it was big. We ran over to make sure no one was in trouble. We didn't see anyone inside, but while we were over there, focused on the fire and waiting for the trucks to get here, Eddie happened to look back. He saw this guy way back over by the equipment trailers, working on getting the doors opened. The man was using bolt cutters to cut the locks off. He was trying to rip us off while we're distracted over here! So Eddie starts yelling and goes running back. Then, out of the blue, some other guy hiding by that lamppost steps out and swings that board over there like a baseball bat." She grimaced. "It was nasty! Eddie never saw it coming. He gets whacked right in the face. He goes down hard. Out cold."

"Shit!" Danny said. "Eddie's the one in the ambulance?"

"Yeah," Kate said, "but he's okay. He's got a broken nose but otherwise he's okay."

Danny blew out his breath slowly.

"So, when he went down, I yelled at the guy, and I started running back to help Eddie. When I got to him, his face was all covered in blood, so I stopped to make sure he could breathe. I was there maybe a minute, two tops. Then, another policeman and I ran over to check on the gear. Those two guys were long gone by then. They made off with our three Red Dragons." She noticed the confused look on Danny's face. "Red . . . digital movie cameras, very expensive. We had three, and they got all three of them. They knew what to look for. It wasn't just a random drug user ripping us off. These guys were pros."

Danny stared at the equipment trailer. "It had to be the Thornes, right? I mean, you offer to pay off the loan next week, and they respond by getting nasty and stealing the cameras."

"It's just like Richard said. They're trying to slow down the film," Toni added.

"That's how I see it," Kate said. "But I got news for them, the bastards. The joke's on them. It won't work. The cameras are insured, and the leasing company has other cameras. They'll put three of 'em on an airplane for us out of LA tomorrow and ship 'em up. We'll lose a day, but we'll be back in business by the first of the week."

Danny nodded. "Good." He watched the firefighters at work for a moment, then he turned to Kate. "Where's Ray?"

Kate shrugged, then she raised an eyebrow. "Not here. Editing, I suppose. At the editor's office."

Danny took a deep breath as he looked into her eyes. "Well . . . one problem at a time, Kate."

She nodded. "I know . . . I'm good. I can see the target."

"Good. You're still on board, then? You're still good for tomorrow?"

"I am." She looked across to the burned out vehicle. The fire was out but smoke and steam still lingered. "You're right. There's no way they're going to let me pay it off. The bastards."

CHAPTER 7

Preserving Evidence

Billy Thorne showed up at the movie set on schedule at eleven a.m. the next morning for his meeting with Kate. By eleven ten, he was gone. Kate hopped out of her trailer where they'd met and walked back to an old Winnebago parked behind her. She reached up and opened the door. "You guys get all that?"

Danny nodded. "Every word. Come on up."

Kate entered and sat next to Toni. The motor home looked like an older, well-used RV from the outside. Inside, it had been gutted and rebuilt with two long desks running the length of the vehicle on either side. In racks above one of the desks, a wall of sophisticated audio and video surveillance gear was mounted.

"We got it all," Kenny said, working on a computer keyboard. "I'm just enhancing the audio a bit now."

"What was all that about Article 14?" Toni asked.

Kate frowned. "That was a complete load of BS, that's what

that was. Danny was right. Thorne said we didn't give them proper notice of our intent to pay them off, and now it's too late. What a load of crap. There's nothing about advance notice in the papers. I could wring his scrawny neck."

"You handled it perfectly," Toni said. "You made it sound like you thought that some local homeless people ripped you off last night for drug money. I think he believed you."

"Good. The little bastard." She turned to Danny. "So now they've said no, I can't pay them back, does this mean that you've got what you need?"

Danny nodded. "Yeah, it does. Not much mistaking their intent now." He turned to Toni. "Well?"

Toni stared at him for a second, then she nodded. "You're right. We've gotta do something."

"Good." He smiled and turned back to Kate. "Congratulations, Kate. You just hired Logan PI. Now we get to work."

* * * *

An hour later, Billy Thorne stepped from between the rhodies on his way from the main house back to his guest house. A small group of white-uniformed gardeners were huddled together near the guest house railing, leaning against their rakes, their attention fixed on something on the ground before them. Billy stopped and stared for a moment, then he clapped his hands loudly. "Hey! Idiots! What's with the standing around? What the hell are you guys doing? We're not paying you morons to waste time on a smoke break!"

The men jumped and split up rapidly, heading back to work—all except one, who remained huddled over the planter, his back to Billy.

"What about you?" Billy demanded as he approached. "You special or something?"

The man turned, and Billy was surprised to see that it was Farley Palmer. He'd been making notes in a small black leather-covered book.

"Special?" Palmer said, standing. "I don't know. My mother thinks so, I suppose, but I really couldn't say. I know I'm definitely no good at yard work."

Billy blinked. "Sorry. I didn't know it was you." He looked at the ground where Farley had been working. "What are you doing there, anyway?"

"I'm preserving evidence."

"What evidence? What is that?"

"It's a footprint. Or, more specifically, it's a shoe print."

"That?" All that was visible was a rectangular mold Farley had built on the ground, about one foot wide and eighteen inches long. It was filled with a plasterlike substance that had apparently just been poured.

"Actually, what you're seeing here is called dental stone. It's used to cast impressions for false teeth. Works well for footprints, too. The track's underneath, of course, in the dirt."

"Is it the intruder's?"

"Very possibly. It's pointed *away* from the deck. I think a gardener working on the planter would more likely stand here, *facing* the planter and the deck. Plus, I talked to a Miss Chloe Rogers up at the house—said she works for you. She said the man that was on your deck jumped over the railing right about here"—he pointed to the rail—"which means he must've landed about here."

He pointed to the casting. "So when I came down here and looked, bingo! There it was, a nice shoe print in the dirt, pretty as you please. It looks fresh to me. And, in addition to it being oriented as it is, it also looks bigger than the shoes that any of your landscapers wear." He looked at Billy's petite shoes. "Bigger than yours, too." He gestured toward the gardeners. "That's why I had 'em all assembled over here, so I could check."

"Their shoe sizes?"

"Yes, their sizes . . . and their faces."

Billy cocked his head.

"As much time as I spent in law enforcement, a lot of times I can tell if a person's lying to me just by studying their face."

"And?"

Farley shrugged. "Nothing. I got nothing from this crowd except that their feet seem too small for this track."

"So you're saying it's *not* one of the gardeners?"

Farley shook his head. "No, I didn't say that. It's certainly possible that one of 'em might be a particularly good liar or might know something, at least. Right now, I'm just forming some initial impressions. That's all."

Billy considered that for a moment, then he pointed toward the footprint. "So what are you going to do with that?"

"I've got a friend who works in the FBI crime lab. He owes

me a favor—more than one, actually. He's waiting for this. Says he can analyze it and tell me the type of shoe and the size."

Billy squinted, then he gave a little smirk. "Type of shoe? So then what? You got a shoe and a size. Big deal. Lots of people wear shoes in this town. Could be anyone. What are you gonna do? Run around like Prince Charming with a glass slipper?"

Farley smiled again. "I admit that it's a long shot. But a lot of police work—investigation work—deals with sorting through clues like this and ruling things out. It's tedious work for sure. But we might get lucky. Who knows? Come to think of it, this wouldn't be the longest shot I ever had that paid off. If the shoe's unique enough, maybe it'll give us a lead that points to some sort of specialty shoe store."

Billy sneered. "Sounds like a lot of work for probably nothin'."

"Yeah—you may be right. But we gotta keep pluggin' away."

THE SETUP

CHAPTER 8

The Grifter

Danny and Toni wheeled into the parking lot of the Edgewater Hotel a couple of minutes before ten a.m. on Monday morning. The Edgewater is a Seattle landmark, built right on top of Pier 67, cantilevered out over the cold water of Puget Sound, where Wall Street runs into Alaskan Way. The hotel is famous for the various rock legends that have stayed there over the years, starting with the Beatles in '64 and extending through today.

They walked through the front doors and made their way through the lobby to Six Seven restaurant, located near the back of the main floor and overlooking Elliott Bay, where they stopped to scan the tables.

"There," Danny said a second later, nodding toward a man seated at a window table on the far side of the restaurant near the water.

The silver-haired man was dressed in gray slacks with a

light blue button-down shirt and a dark red tie. A navy jacket was tossed over the arm of the chair beside him. His sleeves were rolled up casually as he read a copy of *The Seattle Times*. He looked up across the top of his reading glasses as Danny and Toni approached.

"Henry Parker?" Danny said.

The man squinted slightly. "Yeah. Are you Logan?"

Danny nodded. "I am."

Henry stood, and the two men shook hands. "Good to meet you."

Danny turned to Toni. "My partner, Toni Blair."

Henry looked at Toni, and his face softened as he broke into a smile. "Toni Blair," he said, his aqua blue eyes twinkling. "Great name."

Toni smiled as Henry shook her hand. "Thank you, Mr. Parker. May I call you Henry?"

"Well, I'd be disappointed if you didn't." Henry quickly moved around the table and pulled out a chair for Toni. "Here, allow me."

Danny watched the interaction with an amused smile. Henry was easily twice his age, trim, tanned, and quite handsome, just a little shorter than Danny.

"Thank you, sir." She took her seat and looked out across the bay. "Wow, this is beautiful out here."

Immediately south of the hotel, a huge cruise ship was docked at Pier 66, while a half mile farther south, workers were visible at the base of the Seattle Great Wheel, preparing for the day's opening. Beyond the Great Wheel, the Bainbridge Island ferry was slowing for landing at the Colman Dock ferry terminal.

"You know, I've lived here my whole life," Toni said, "and I've never been to this restaurant. Didn't even know it was here. There's, like, this whole other world out here on the water."

"It's spectacular, isn't it?" Henry said. He scanned the bay. "You know, they call this place the 'Rain City'. But today? Not so much. When the sun's out, there's no better place in the world than Seattle—and I mean none. I lived here for a time a few years back, you know? My sister Mary *still* lives up here. I like to visit." He turned back to them. "At least in the summer when it's not raining."

"We wanted to thank you for dropping everything and coming up to meet us on such short notice," Toni said. "Richard speaks very highly of you."

Henry chuckled, pushed a breakfast plate out of the way, and leaned back from the table. "Yeah, well, there I was, sitting out on my patio reading the *Times*, and out of the blue, Richard calls. Wow! Richard friggin' Taylor from Seattle. Talk about a voice from the past. I hadn't talked to Richard in years, and I gotta admit"—he lowered his voice—"as I'm sure he explained, Richard and I didn't always see eye to eye back in the day. The man caused me no end of grief while he was with the police department. There was a time when I would *not* have been pleased to hear from him—by telephone or otherwise."

He grinned. "But times change, right? We had a nice little talk for a bit. Joked about the old days. He told me about his retirement from the force and his PI business—" he looked at Danny, "–which I understand he then sold to you. Then he proceeded to lay out a story about how the PI firm of yours is wrapped up in a problem that he thinks I just might have an interest in—maybe I could provide a little help. 'Come on up,' he said. 'The weather's great.'"

He looked out across the water. "He got that part right. So I told him, 'Why not? I can check in on Mary. And while I'm there, I'll talk to your friends.'" He smiled. "So voilà! Got in late yesterday afternoon. Had dinner with an old friend, and now, here I am: Henry Parker, at your service."

"Well, thanks," Danny said.

"My pleasure. Richard said you guys are working with a client who's got themselves caught in a trap set by a particularly nasty little pond scum I happen to be familiar with, man by the name of Frank Thorne."

Danny gave a slight tilt of his head. "You know about Frank Thorne, then?"

Henry's eyes narrowed. "You could say that, yeah. Frank Thorne killed my brother-in-law."

* * * *

"Either of you ever hear the name Harold Van Tuyl?"

"Harold Van Tuyl . . ." Danny shook his head. "Doesn't sound familiar to me."

"Me neither," Toni said.

Henry shrugged. "Well, it doesn't matter—he's dead now. Besides, you probably wouldn't have heard of Harold unless you.

were in the real estate business anyway. Harold was Mary's husband, my brother-in-law. He was a good man—smart, honest, hardworking, very successful real estate developer here in Seattle back in the day. Started small with houses, ended up building shopping centers. He put up buildings all over Puget Sound. Man was a dynamo. Problem was, like a lot of those builder types, he couldn't quit. He had building in his blood—it was like a disease. He had plenty of money—house, cars, boat, the whole ticket. But he kept at it, long past the time he should have hung it up and sat back and enjoyed life." He grimaced. "So anyway, here's old Harold, doing his building thing in 2005, 2006. He had himself a few big developments underway—two or three, I think. Everybody's happy, and then one day, *BANG!* 2008 comes along, and the real estate market crashes. Over the next couple of years, his construction lenders went belly up, just like a string of dominos. Nothing to do with Harold or his projects, but the banks just evaporated—gone. And I'm not talking about neighborhood credit unions either. These were big banks, national outfits. They all ended up getting taken over by the FDIC, who naturally, being feds, refused to honor the loan commitments the original banks made to Harold. So, poof! No more money for his projects."

He took a sip of water. "As you might imagine, that was a problem. The buildings were halfway finished, and suddenly there was no money to pay people to finish 'em. Since they weren't done, Harold couldn't lease 'em out and pay off the loans that the feds were now holding. The buildings *had* to get finished. So Harold dipped into his personal money, started feeding the projects himself, trying to get 'em done. Good idea, but then again, these were good-sized projects—big suckers, tens of millions of dollars each. You know, those trendy outdoor malls with the expensive stores.

"It wasn't long before even a wealthy guy like Harold was tapped out. So he did what developers always do when they get in trouble. He started scrambling—selling things, taking out loans, whatever. He basically went hunting for money to finish. But things kept getting worse. Got so bad that the only money to be had was from the hard-money lenders and the loan sharks—bottom feeders—guys who'd happily charge you ten points up front plus twenty percent interest and still want your firstborn as collateral."

"Guys like Frank Thorne," Danny said.

"Exactly. Enter Frank Thorne. Biggest mistake of Harold's life. But truth be told, by then Harold was up against it. It was either borrow the money from the sharks, pay the price, and hope for the best, or else go under right then and there. In hindsight, he should have just bitten the bullet and given the feds the projects back and called it a day. But no, Harold was a developer, and developers are eternal optimists. Harold convinced himself that the market was gonna stabilize—improve, even. Everything was gonna get better. So he went ahead and tapped the hard-money source.

"Of course, the market *didn't* get better. It kept getting worse, way worse than anyone could have ever seen. It eventually tanked altogether. Shopping centers became worth literally pennies on the dollar. And Harold ended up seriously overextended. He ran out of cash, and then he ran out of answers." He grimaced. "And that was Frank Thorne's cue. He started moving in. He started putting the big-time squeeze on Harold.

"At first, Harold tried to be responsible. Mary says he met with Thorne numerous times, explained the situation, told Thorne he couldn't pay him, and offered up workout plans instead—alternatives, you know? And Thorne, he was sly. He pretended to be reasonable. In fact, the first thing he did was offer to loan Harold even *more* money. But that was a trap. When Harold took advantage, Thorne used that as an excuse to get Harold to put liens on all his other properties, along with documents that said that if *any* of the properties defaulted, the loans on *all of them* defaulted. The bastard was completely settin' Harold up. He knew Harold was going under, so he decided to give him a great big shove."

Henry paused, grabbed his juice glass, and took a drink.

"So, sure enough, Harold ended up defaulting, and Thorne jumped in and foreclosed on all the properties—eventually forced Harold and Mary into personal bankruptcy. Whatever Frank Thorne didn't cherry-pick for himself, the courts ended up taking—everything that Harold and Mary worked thirty years to put together. Real estate, cash, personal assets, even their house. They had a fabulous house on Hunts Point, which Richard says you're familiar with."

Danny's eyes widened. "You wouldn't happen to mean 4209 Hunts Point Road?"

"That's the one. That used to be Harold and Mary's house."

"You're kidding," Toni said.

"Nope, not kidding. Thorne's apparently kept that one for himself."

He stared out at the bay for a moment, then, without turning back, he continued. "Losing the house was sort of the beginning of the end for Harold. After Thorne foreclosed on them and forced them into bankruptcy, he and Mary moved to a little rental house over in Lakeside—it was all they could afford. Harold had a helluva time trying to shift mental gears. He tried to find work, but what was he gonna do? This was what, 2011, 2012? Harold was a sixty-five-year-old failed shopping center developer at a time when the shopping center industry was knocked on its ass. There wasn't much call for a man with his talents."

He sniffed. "He tried to keep his head above water, but eventually he just gave up. One morning real early, he went for a ride. Drove out to Redmond. Parked at one of his shopping centers that had been foreclosed on. Pulled out a .38 and blew his brains out. Left Mary a widow." He shook his head and sighed. "The dumbass. I can understand why he did it, but I sure as hell can't forgive him. Now, Mary's the one left behind. She's a shadow of her former self, like a shell. All these years later, and she's still struggling, trying to piece things back together."

Henry turned from the window to face Toni and Danny. "So, there you have it. The way I see it: Harold's responsible for pulling the trigger. But make no mistake—that bastard Frank Thorne's the son of a bitch who put the gun in his hand." He took a deep breath. "Anyway, now you know why it is that I would 'drop everything,' as you put it, and fly up to sunny Seattle."

Toni nodded. "I'm sorry your sister had to go through all that."

"Me, too." It was silent for a few seconds, then Henry smiled, his face seeming to relax. "So tell me about this painting you're trying to recover."

"*Lys dans de Champs de Moret* by Alfred Sisley," Toni said.

Henry raised an eyebrow. "*C'est celui-là. Est-ce utile?*"

Toni smiled. "*Oui, deux millions de dollars, peut-être plus—si c'était réel.*"

Henry's eyes opened wider for a moment. "I see."

Danny looked from one to the other. "Sorry, I got a D in French."

Toni laughed. "Henry asked if the painting is valuable. I told him it certainly is, at two million, maybe more—if only it were real."

"Or maybe just five grand as is," Danny said.

"Two million or five grand," Henry said. "I can see where Thorne might find that, uh . . . troubling—if he knew about it." He chuckled. "But I gotta say I like the predicament it puts him in. And the opportunity it gives us."

"So it's something that might interest you?" Danny asked.

Henry rubbed his chin. "I'm not going to lie to ya—in general, there's nothing I like better than relieving a greedy bastard of a portion of his ill-gotten gains. I've made a good career of it. And make no mistake, I'd *especially* like to take a crack at Frank Thorne, for reasons that I've explained. But as much as I'd like to set him back a peg or two, I—*we'd*—need to be careful—*very* careful. Frank Thorne is a dangerous man. And if you two have done your homework, and you strike me as the types that have, then you must know that if we do this, we're going to not just be yanking the tiger by the tail, we're going to be kicking him square in the nuts—pardon my language. He's not gonna like it, not one little bit. You two ready for that?"

"Within reason," Danny said. "I mean, we wouldn't want to have to kill anybody or anything like that in order to protect ourselves, but we talked it over. We're aware of the risks."

Henry raised an eyebrow. "Interesting way of looking at things. Never had to kill anyone myself. Let me think on it for a day, come up with a few possibilities we can kick around. I'll make a phone call, bring in my executive team."

"You have an executive team?" Toni asked.

"Yeah. Me, my daughter, Lulu, and Johnny Redmond, her fiancé, who also happens to be my number one guy. I trust 'em both."

"You think you guys can come up with something?" Danny asked. "Something to get the painting back without the Thorne's catching on?"

Henry thought for a couple of seconds, then he said, "Sure—there's always an angle. In all the years I've been at this game, one thing I've learned you can always count on is the power that greed has over a man like Frank Thorne. It takes over... makes 'em blind... makes 'em do things they ordinarily wouldn't. And all that makes them predictable—at least a little. We can work with that."

Toni tilted her head. "From what you just said, it sounds like it could also make them dangerous."

Henry turned to her. "That's true. But we're careful. We have a little saying that our group goes by—keeps us out of trouble."

"Yeah?"

Henry smiled, his blue eyes sparkling. "Yep. Move fast, stay one step ahead."

CHAPTER 9

Table for Four

The posh Overlake Golf & Country Club restaurant on Lake Washington was crowded with the Medina and Bellevue elite—the doctors, lawyers, and businessmen who made things happen on the east side. The crowd, mostly men, talked and laughed boisterously, and all seemed to be enjoying themselves. The large sliding glass doors onto the patio had been rolled open to let the members enjoy the late-afternoon summer breeze flowing up from the eighteenth green. At a secluded table near the back of the room, Farley Palmer was seated with Frank and Billy Thorne and Doyle Reese.

Farley turned a page in his small notebook, then looked up at Frank. "I've gone over every inch of the exterior of the property, sir. So far, I have to report that there's only limited physical evidence. In fact, all I've found is a single shoe print by the guest house and some scuff marks at the beach where it looks like the boat landed."

"What about the cameras?" Frank said as he shoveled a forkful of crab salad into his mouth. "You check those out? I spent a fortune putting them friggin' cameras up all over the place this summer. I'm surprised we didn't see the dude."

"You would think," Farley said. "Unfortunately, though, your cameras aren't monitored. No one sits in front of the monitors on a routine basis. The feed goes straight to a hard drive."

"We don't have that kinda manpower, boss," Doyle said.

Frank looked at him, then turned to Farley. "But there's still gotta be something on the recordings. You can still check 'em now, right?"

"I have. I reviewed the footage from *all* your cameras. No sign of the intruder on any of them. I will say that none of the cameras cover the lawn or anywhere down near the beach."

Doyle pursed his lips and said, "We didn't figure anybody'd come from that way. What about the guest house? That's where the guy was seen. I know we had a camera put in down there."

Farley snuck a quick glance at Billy before responding. "That's correct, there is a camera on the eaves that overlooks the guest house deck. But I checked that one, too, and there hasn't been any footage recorded by that particular camera since the first of the summer. It's been disconnected."

Frank paused, fork suspended in midair. Then he turned and glared at Billy.

Billy shrank in his chair. "Sorry, Pop. Damn thing's pointed right at the hot tub. Sometimes, things get a little, uh, active there. I don't want Ernie or Theo sittin' up at the big house gettin' their jollies watchin' me doin' some . . . entertaining."

Frank glared at Billy for another moment, then he turned back to Farley. "So, no clues."

"Oh no, sir," Farley said. "I didn't mean to say there were no clues. I said there was 'limited physical evidence.' There's a difference."

Frank lifted an eyebrow. "Don't play word games with me, Palmer."

Farley shook his head. "Wouldn't think of it, sir. Like I said, the only *physical* evidence that I've found so far is the shoe print. And with that, I've made a casting and sent it to a friend at the FBI crime lab. He's doing me a favor and running it to determine the type of shoe and the size. There's a chance—a slim chance, but a chance nonetheless—that the shoe might tell us something about the intruder. But aside from the physical evidence, there's other evidence as well. We have witness testimony from a Miss Chloe Rogers, although, in truth, we have to take what she says with a grain of salt."

"Why would that be?"

"Uh . . ." Billy said, "Chloe saw the guy, but she was drunk—too much champagne. She doesn't remember what he looked like."

Frank looked at him. "Why am I not surprised?" He turned to Farley. "Go on."

"To be fair," Farley said, "it was dark, and the man was apparently camouflaged. Miss Rogers said she believes the man was Caucasian with his face painted dark. But there's virtually no chance she could ever identify him, even had she not been .

. . impaired. In addition to what Miss Rogers saw on the deck, we also know that both she and Billy observed the man running from the property," Farley said, referring to his notebook. "Both agree that the man was tall, thin, and quite athletic—apparently a very fast runner. Based on the way the boat left the beach, we believe it likely was piloted by a second individual who was waiting." Farley flipped a couple of pages in his notebook. "Judging by the scuff marks on the beach, the boat was most likely a rigid-bottom inflatable, probably one of those with a fiberglass or aluminum hull, twenty to thirty feet long with two, perhaps three, outboard engines. Some boats of this type are very powerful—the military uses them. I've started checking with rental outfits along the lake, but so far, there aren't very many who rent such a craft, and no one I talked to rented such a boat overnight last week."

"So, gimme the bottom line here," Frank said. "Where you going with this? You think you're gonna be able to ID the bastard or not?"

"Truthfully, sir, I think it's a long shot. I mean, you got your basic lack of witnesses, plus a shortage of hard evidence. It means that it'll be tough to solve this using your standard methods. But there are other ways."

"Again, speak English, Palmer," Frank said.

"Sorry, sir. What I mean is, instead of trying to come up with a suspect based on a limited stack of evidence, we can always work backward and focus on motives instead. *Why* would somebody want to do this? Once we figure out the why, then we reexamine the physical evidence we have, and we can develop a profile and see if a suspect pops out. It's possible we could get lucky."

"Or we can just drop it, boss," Doyle said. "Save the money." He turned to Farley. "No offense."

Farley smiled. "None taken."

Frank thought for a second. "Nah, I don't want to toss in the towel, not yet anyway. There's too much at risk to just drop it." He paused for a moment, surveying the crowd. A moment later, he said, "So we ain't quittin'. Palmer, get back out there and dig a little harder. I ain't payin' you to come up with a bunch of bullshit theories. I want answers. Find out who did this."

Farley gave him a thin smile. "Yes, *sir*!"

* * * *

Frank watched Farley walk away from the table. "Ya hear how he said that? 'Yes, *sir*.' Man's got an attitude. There's something 'bout him—the way he looks at me, the way he answers questions—like he knows something I don't know. Sort of like he thinks he's the smartest guy in the room. I don't like him."

Doyle laughed. "That's okay, boss. I don't think he likes you neither."

"Why the hell do you use him, then?" Billy asked.

Frank shrugged. "Sometimes you gotta do things you don't like. Palmer's good, the best at what he does. If anyone can find something, he can."

Frank scanned the room, then he reached into his pocket and pulled out a small black case.

Doyle eyed it immediately. "That what I'm thinking it is?"

"If you're thinkin' it's an engagement ring, then yeah." He opened the case and placed it on the table. "Gonna be, anyway, once I get a new band for it. It's going out to the jewelers in the morning."

"Holy crap!!" Doyle said. "Would you look at that?"

The huge diamond, set in a simple gold setting, scattered the beam from the overhead light into a million tiny flames of color.

"Seven-point-two carats," Frank said. "Flawless. You recognize it?"

Doyle nodded. "Yeah, of course. It was McPherson's wife's."

"That's right," Frank said. "Ugly woman. Had fingers fatter than yours. They can't even resize the damn thing. They gotta take the stone off and get a new band to fit Lorraine."

"Well, it's damn nice lookin', Frank," Doyle said. "And congratulations are in order?"

Frank nodded smugly. "Soon. Gonna pop the question when I get it back in a couple of weeks."

Billy stared at the ring without expression until, several moments later, he looked up and noticed Frank eyeing him. He forced a smile. "Uh, yeah, Pop," he said. "I'm speechless, here. But the ring—wow! It's off the chart."

CHAPTER 10

The Mob

"So, in summary, the results of our research show quite conclusively that as we modulate the pectin network of a plant epidermis, we develop the ability to significantly impact the compressive elastic modulus of fully hydrated primary plant cell walls." The professor spoke with a thick Irish brogue. He paused and glanced up from his notes. "You two got all that?"

Two female grad students—one blonde, one redhead—sat across from him, both furiously tapping away on tablet keyboards. "Geez, give us half a second, will ya, Professor?" one of them said without looking up.

"Sure." The professor's office was small, bookshelves on the wall behind him overflowing with thick textbooks and binders full of research notes. His desk was equally crowded. The door to the office was propped open, and the sign on the door read:

Dr. Conner Farrell, PhD
Senior Lecturer
School of Biomolecular Science
University College, Dublin

He stood up and walked over to his window while he waited for his assistants to catch up. Outside, the sun was shining, the breeze gentle, the temperature warm. It was a beautiful summer day in Dublin in mid-August. A few students took advantage of the sunshine, seated in the shade beneath the trees, laughing and talking, throwing a Frisbee here, kicking a soccer ball over there.

"Ladies," he said, "I hate to rush you, but I'm about to lose—" He stopped in midsentence when the text message alert on his phone chimed. He saw that it was from Henry Parker. *Hi, professor. Got a job for us in Seattle. Kickoff next Monday. Two weeks tops. Good wages. You in?*

The professor read the note again. He flipped through the pages on the calendar on his desk. "Two weeks from next Monday," he whispered, counting off the days. "I'd be home on Sunday, September 6." He looked up. "The new term starts on Tuesday the eighth, right?"

Both assistants nodded in unison. "Aye."

A slow smile started to spread across his face. He turned around. "Ladies?"

They continued typing without looking up.

"Hey!" he said.

This time, they stopped typing.

"I'm afraid something's come up rather unexpectedly." He

closed his briefcase. "I need to be leaving ya for a bit." He started packing his briefcase.

* * * *

Sleeks Day Spa was located on East 54th Street in Midtown Manhattan, halfway between Lexington and Park Avenue. The heavy front door was distinguished and slightly understated—it looked expensive.

Inside, the lobby was crowded with well-dressed, mostly middle-aged women checking in at the front desk, then reading the latest fashion magazines while they waited to be escorted back for an hour or two of indulgence.

"Muriel?" a handsome dark-haired man called out. "Muriel?"

A silver-haired woman looked up. "I'm Muriel," she said, standing and eyeing the man warily. She made no move to come forward. "But you're not Manolo."

The man smiled. "No, I'm not." He pointed to his name tag. "I'm Salvatore DeVito, but everyone calls me Sal."

"Where's Manolo?" Muriel protested. "I always work with Manolo."

"Muriel," the silver-haired woman at the counter said, "Manolo called in sick this morning. Sal's one of our best. I asked him if he could handle Manolo's clients, just for today. Is that all right?"

Muriel hesitated. "I...don't...Doris, does he know Swedish?"

Doris nodded.

Sal smiled. "Do I know Swedish? Muriel, I may as well have grown up in Stockholm." He paused when his phone beeped to indicate a text message. Muriel scowled at him.

"I am so sorry, Muriel. I was in such a hurry to meet you, I forgot to turn my phone off. Let me just..." He reached for the phone and started to turn it off but stopped short when he saw the message from Henry Parker. *Sal, how's it going? Got a job for us in Seattle. Kickoff next Monday. Two weeks. Good wages. You in?*

He drew a short deep breath before turning to look at Doris. She raised an eyebrow, questioning. Sal smiled and gave her a quick nod.

Doris turned to Muriel. "You know, Muriel, on second thought, I think I might have someone you might like even better, a real Swedish expert. I think we'll have something really special for you today."

"But... but..." Muriel stuttered.

Doris walked around from behind the front desk. "Come on over here, dear. Let's go back. I'll introduce you to Ingrid, and we can show you what we have planned."

* * * *

The sign on the man's desk read:

Je'Von Coleman
Sr. Probation Officer
Cook County

The man, tall and balding, had reading classes perched on the end of his nose. He leaned back as he studied the report in front of him, flipping from one page to the next.

"Hmm," he said, shaking his head slowly. "I'll be damned." He read some more before looking up at the man seated across from him. "Well, you did it. I don't know how, but you did it. Says here I'm to move you from active supervision to inactive supervision, effective immediately. Says that since you're now down to financial remuneration only, you don't even need to check in anymore." He set the report down for a moment. "What a crock."

The man on the other side of Coleman's desk was dressed in crisp business attire—a precisely fitted dark navy Brooks Brothers Madison suit with a light blue shirt and a dark blue striped tie, gold cuff links, and black, highly polished wing tips. He was of medium build, and his silver and brown hair was combed neatly backward. He looked like any one of a thousand other successful white businessmen on LaSalle Street in the heart of Chicago's financial district.

He smiled. "Come on now, Je'Von, I *told* you I was going to talk to my lawyer and ask him to file a motion to amend the order. I did, he did, and the court agreed. You can't get pissed now."

Coleman stared at him. "Pissed? Who's pissed? One less file for me to be concerned with." He shrugged as he stamped the file. "Must be a helluva good lawyer," he mumbled. He stamped two more pages, then he read the next page before looking up.

"Cameron Greer, aka Buttons Greer, says here I'm supposed to remind you that even though you got yourself a hot-shit lawyer and you gamed the system, and even though you're no longer subject to in-person supervision, your obligation to pay that fine"—he smiled—"that big-assed twenty-thousand-dollar fine, is still there."

"It says that?"

Coleman stopped smiling. "I'm paraphrasing. It also says you got to do it inside of six months, else the sheriff will come looking for ya. Which means your smug ass will be right back in that chair. And that"—he smiled broadly—"is something I'm personally lookin' forward to." He stood. "Ticktock, ticktock, Mr. Greer."

Greer started to stand as well. "Well, if that'll do it . . ."

Coleman nodded. "Yeah, one other thing. You also know that your no-travel order is still valid. You take one step outside of Cook County before you pay off that big, hefty fine, and your probation package unravels. You'll be spending the next six months in the county lockup."

Greer smiled. "I guess I'd better not let that happen, right?" Just at that moment, his phone buzzed, announcing a text message.

"Ahem," Coleman said, nodding to the No Cell Phones sign on the wall beside him. "Rules still apply in here."

"Not a phone call," Greer said quickly as he pulled the phone from his jacket pocket. "It's a text."

He quickly scanned the message from Henry Parker. *Hi, Buttons. Ferguson told me you're cleared off supervised status. Good news. Better news—got a job for us in Seattle. Kickoff next Monday. Two weeks. Good wages. You in?*

Greer smiled. Coleman frowned.

"Something you want to share, Mr. Greer?"

Buttons chuckled as he put the phone back in his pocket. "Well, as a matter of fact, it's good news, Je'Von. I just got a job offer. Looks like I might be able to pay that big old fine after all. Hell, maybe even ahead of time."

Coleman gave him an evil smile. "Isn't that nice? You'd best be careful now, Mr. Greer."

* * * *

"*Anata no ashimoto o mitekudasai.*" The silver-haired Japanese man in the dark green tour guide vest stepped forward to help an elderly woman negotiate the step from the hotel shuttle bus down to the sidewalk. He beamed as he reached out to help her. "Watch your step, okay?"

"*Arigatou gozaimasu,*" the old woman said, smiling and blushing slightly as she reached for the handsome gentleman's hand.

He turned to his assistant, a younger man. "Koji, would you help her down?"

After the group's guide had assembled the remaining tourists, he and his assistant herded the group toward a Pacific-Asian tour bus with a bright Universal Studios advertisement on the side. The tourists chatted happily amongst themselves as they began to load onto the bus.

"Tanaka-san! Tanaka-san!"

The tour guide turned to see a young woman running towards him from the office door. "You left your phone!" she called to him, waving the phone. "It's been buzzing all morning."

Automatically, he reached down and patted his pockets. "*Shimatta!*" he muttered. She was right. He met her in the middle of the driveway. "Thank you, Rosie."

"No problem. Dad says he has another group for you guys this afternoon."

"Good." He looked at his phone and saw that he had a new text message from Henry Parker. *Shinbone, ohayō. I've got a job for you and Koji in Seattle. Kickoff next Monday. Two weeks. Good wages. You in?*

He froze in place.

"What is it, Shinichi?" Rosie asked.

Koji walked over to him. "What's up, boss?"

Shinichi looked at him and smiled broadly. "Business opportunity."

Koji raised an eyebrow. Shinichi gave a slight smile and a quick nod, causing Koji to lean forward and give him a quiet victory fist pump. "Yes!" he whispered.

Rosie looked on in confusion.

"Ah, Rosie," Shinichi said, "please tell your father for us that Koji and I just got called away on a special assignment for which we must prepare. We are required to leave at once."

"Called away?" She looked at the two, then at the bus, then back. "Leave? What do you mean? You're leaving? Now?"

"Yes." He looked past her into the lobby. "We have to pack. I believe Hirano-san there is looking for something to do. He can take this group. We must leave now."

"Now? But . . . how long will you be gone? What about the

group this afternoon?"

"Two weeks," Shinichi said, unbuttoning his dark green Pacific-Asian Tours vest. "Your father will understand. We have an arrangement."

CHAPTER 11

Kickoff

Rain from a fast-moving afternoon thundershower beat against the living room window of Henry's suite at the Evergreen just before noon the following Monday. The room was crowded with a dozen people. The furniture had been pushed to the side so that every possible chair, sofa, and ottoman was arranged into a large U shape. The end tables and the coffee tables in the center were crowded with water bottles and canned soft drinks. Kenny had set up a projector, pointed at a wall where the hotel-art piece had been removed. A large photo of Farley Palmer—the one Kate had grabbed with her cell phone—was being projected.

"Henry," Conner Farrell said, nodding toward the photo, "if this guy's as good a detective as Richard says he is, is that not a cause for concern?"

"How's that?"

"I mean, you say you want to include Logan and his crew in the con, which, by the way, I agree would ordinarily make sense—trusted local, verifiable reputation, so on. The problem, as I see it, is that if Danny's acting as a front man for us, and"—he nodded toward the screen—"if this Farley Palmer guy is somehow able to independently connect him to Kate Morgan because of some prior event, well, then, he's gonna get suspicious, right? It might be just a little too coincidental."

Henry nodded. "Good point. And it's something we've focused on." He turned to Danny. "I know we've been through this, but for the sake of everyone else, is there any way that Thorne or Palmer can connect you to Kate, the film, or the painting?"

Danny shook his head. "No, I don't believe so. I've seen Kate a total of four times since I got out of the army." He counted off on his fingers. "First, I bumped into her at Starbucks a couple of weeks ago. That was completely random, and there's no way that's a vulnerability. Next was the next day, the morning after the midnight boat trip to Hunts Point. I suppose the Thornes could have had someone at the movie set watching, but they'd have had to get up and get organized pretty damn early, because our meeting was at nine a.m. I doubt they could have set up that fast. Possible, but remote. A week or so later, we were on set, but we never got out of our motor home. We couldn't have been seen, even if they were looking. And the last time was the night they set the car on fire. I suppose they could have had someone there watching, but by the time we got there, the place was crawling with cops. They searched the whole area fairly thoroughly and found nothing. I don't think Thorne's guys hung around afterward long enough to see who showed up."

Henry started to speak, but the short, red-haired young woman seated beside him went first. "Guys, me and Dad and Johnny went through the whole story minute by minute with Danny and Toni. We looked for every instance where there might be some connection."

"Lulu's right," Johnny Redmond added. He was seated next to Lulu. "We think we're clear. But we are on the same page about maintaining separation between Danny and Kate in the future. That means no more visits from Danny and his team to the movie set. And no visits from Kate to the Logan PI office. We should be good."

Henry nodded. "Guys, we all know Thorne could be dangerous. Move fast—one step ahead, right? So if we see Thorne's start to connect the dots, we'll fold up the con. Won't be safe for any of us." He turned to Danny. "Especially you."

Danny nodded. "Or Kate."

* * * *

Four miles away, Kate watched as the company wrapped up the final seconds of a dramatic scene featuring a serious confrontation between the two main characters of *Fade to Crimson*. When the action finished, Ray called out, "Cut!" followed a second later by, "Great work, everyone!" A few members of the crew applauded.

Kate smiled and clapped.

"You're hard at it, I see."

She jumped and turned quickly to see Farley Palmer standing behind her. "Excuse me?" she said, taking a step back.

"Ms. Morgan," the man said with a smile, "I'm sorry I startled you. I was afraid to make any noise because of the filming over there. Ah... anyway, you might remember me—my name's Farley Palmer. I'm a private investigator and I've been hired to look into someone sneaking on to an expensive estate at Hunts Point a couple of weeks ago. I was with Billy Thorne when he visited you the day afterwards."

"I remember you."

His smile grew wider. "Good. I can see you're busy here, but I didn't get a chance to talk to you during our first visit, and I wonder, if it's not too much trouble, if I could bother you with just a couple of questions now."

* * * *

"Henry," Buttons said, "I'm sure you've considered this, but whatever we decide to run, it needs to start with a good hook, right? We need a great setup. We need a great con, something that'll catch this guy's interest enough to make him want to give up that painting. So what do we know about this Frank Thorne character? Got any weaknesses we can use? Drugs? Booze? Women?"

Henry shook his head. "First off, keep in mind that it's *Billy* Thorne who seems to be running lead on this, not Frank. Frank Thorne may be standing behind the curtain, probably is, for that matter. But I think we gotta go through Billy first. That means, for now at least, Billy Thorne's our mark."

"Along those lines, from what we've been able to piece together," Danny said, "Billy Thorne seems well protected. Papa Frank seems to be fully aware of Billy's . . . proclivities. So he keeps him well-looked-after, even to the point where it looks like Billy has a full-time bodyguard/babysitter to keep him out of trouble."

"That's gonna make it a little tougher to get to him," Buttons said.

"True," Johnny said. "But not impossible. Everyone has a weakness."

"So what's his?" Sal asked. "How do we approach him? Is he a gambler?"

"Ah," Kenny said. "He likes the ponies."

The room fell silent as all eyes shifted to Kenny as if he'd uttered the magic words.

"Danny's had me and Doc following him every day since we got involved. Billy's only missed two days at Emerald Downs out of the past ten days. He and that bodyguard guy go down there most every afternoon that the horses are running. You might be able to get to him there."

"He's a bettor?" Henry asked.

Kenny nodded. "We followed behind him a few times. He bets pretty big. Mostly, he loses."

Henry stared at the screen, then he nodded slowly. After a moment, he said, "It's comin' to me . . . how about we use a fluttering bird? From what I'm hearing, he seems like the type where that might work."

Sal raised his eyebrows. "You mean there at the track?"

"Yep."

Buttons smiled. "Lemme guess who you're thinkin' the bird's gonna be." He looked toward Toni.

She looked at Buttons for a moment, then she shifted to Henry. "What's a fluttering bird?"

"Pretty maiden in distress," he said, smiling. "You'll be perfect."

Toni tilted her head.

Henry turned to Danny. "Any objections? You'd be part of it, too. You two care to be our ropers?"

Danny tilted his head. "Tell me again what we do as ropers."

"Ropers are part of what we call the setup. We build a whole story–you'll both be part of it."

"We'll be seen? Public?" Danny asked. "They'd be able to check us out."

"Yeah," Henry said. "That's the beauty of using locals for ropers. The marks will have someone they can actually look in to. It give's 'em someone they think they can rely on."

"But they'll know who we are," Danny said.

"Yes, they will. But we'll set it up so they're convinced you're on their side."

"How will we know what to say or do?" Toni asked.

Henry smiled. "We'll work out the story, trust me. Ever done any acting?"

Toni shook her head. "No."

"Well," Henry said, "it doesn't matter. You'll do great. The bottom line is that we want to have the mark approach us, instead of the other way around. When he sees you, that's pretty much a given. He makes the first move. That way, he thinks it's his idea. He's not so wary."

Danny smiled. "The fluttering bird."

"Exactly," Henry said. "The bird's the bait. Then the roper hooks him. The mark doesn't see us coming."

* * * *

"Okay," Kate said from the doorway of her motor home office. "One more time, then you're out of here. The night of the eleventh, I was home, sleeping. Neither Ray nor I had anything to do with your burglar." She laughed. "You said they came in by boat? That's funny. Neither of us knows how to drive a boat."

Farley scribbled in his notebook. "No . . . boat. I got it." He shrugged. "I'm sorry to have bothered you—you've been very helpful. I think I've got everything I need."

"Good. You know, Mr. Palmer, your client is a liar and a cheat. Did you know that I tried to pay off the loan, and he said no?"

"Uh . . . no, I was not aware."

"Yeah. Well, it seems like Billy's got you running around doing his bidding, but he doesn't really trust you with the whole inside story, does he?"

Farley didn't answer, so Kate continued. "When you talk to him, feel free to tell him I'm not going to sit still. I'm having my lawyer check it out. Just for the record, Mr. Palmer, we're not in the habit of ripping off the people who fund our films—even Billy Thorne. That would make it kind of hard to stay in business, don't you think?"

Farley smiled. "Got to admit, it makes sense to me. Thank you, ma'am." He reached into a pocket. "Why don't you keep one of my business cards? Just in case you remember something else."

* * * *

"I got one," Buttons said quickly. "A little obvious maybe, but what if we play him on a bad-loan con? Loans being the family business and all. He'll be at ease."

Henry shook his head. "*He* might, but *I* won't. Billy Thorne's our mark, but we gotta assume *Frank* Thorne's watching over this deal. Frank's forgotten more about loan rip-offs than we'll ever know. Hell, he practically wrote the book on 'em. He'll see a bad-loan con from a mile away."

"How about internet gaming?" the professor asked. "That seems to be the rage nowadays. One of those things where you go online and you place bets against one another. We could program something, set him up just like on the wire, except we use a sports-bet con instead."

"We thought about that," Henry said. "But there are a few problems, starting with the fact that none of us are computer programmers. Plus, we don't know if he bets on sport games and, if so, how much. We know he bets at the track, but we have no evidence to suggest he's a sports gambler. Might not be his cup of tea." He turned back to the group. "What else, guys?"

The room was quiet for several moments while Henry waited for ideas from the team members, but they simply looked back without suggestions.

Finally, Sal said, "C'mon, Henry. You're playing with us. You brought this *particular* group of us together for a reason. We've all got a particular set of skills that you need so we know you guys must have something cooked up. You always do. So spill."

Henry looked at him a moment, then he gave a little shrug. "Maybe. I'm trying to keep you guys on your toes, keep you sharp. But you're right—it could be we have a little something we're working up."

"I knew it!"

"What is it?" the professor asked.

Henry smiled. "So the Thornes fancy themselves as businesspeople, right? They're crooks to be sure, but crooks with a business flare. Even got an office in downtown Seattle. Judging by the way they seem to be acting, they're keen on having it at least look like they've gone legit these days—fancy digs, lunch at the country club, box seats at the track, the whole package. So, that bein' the case, how 'bout we run 'em on a ground-floor con? Give 'em something that lets 'em think they're the smartest guys in the room—the next Apple computer, the next Google— something that lets 'em think they're one up on their neighbors."

"What do you have in mind?" the professor said.

Henry smiled. "I'm thinkin' of a little thing we're calling the Hustle. It's a . . . " He paused as a gust of wind and rain rattled the window. "I think I'm gonna change the name —call it the Rain City Hustle."

"The Rain City Hustle," Sal said slowly, as if trying the words on. "Rolls out kinda nice."

Lulu began passing out a printout with a green and gold logo on top. "Boys," she said, "welcome to the ground floor: Emerald Fusion Technology."

"We're going into the renewable-energy business, fellas," Henry said. "We get up and running and dangle it in front of Thorne, he'll want in so bad he'll practically throw the painting at us."

"Fusion?" the professor asked.

Henry nodded. "Yep. Office, lab—the whole works. Which means we're gonna need a store."

* * * *

Danny's phone vibrated, alerting him to a new text. He pulled it out and read the message. It was from Kate. *Danny-Farley Palmer just left. Snooping around, asking questions about the other night. Told him nothing. Obviously.*

Toni reached over and turned his phone her way. After reading the text, she whispered to Danny, "That was timely. You going to tell Henry?"

Danny looked at the front of the room, where Henry continued to talk about the operation. After a few moments, he shook his head. "No. No need. Palmer's fishing. That's to be expected. There's nothing to tell."

CHAPTER 12

World Headquarters

A day later, Danny and Kenny drove through the north end of Bellevue, west of the multiple buildings that made up the sprawling Microsoft campus between I-520 and Bel-Red Road. Just past a row of light industrial buildings, Kenny pointed and said, "Right turn up there—between the bottling company and the school-bus parking lot."

Danny made the turn, and they drove an additional two hundred yards before reaching the end of the road, where they slowed, then stopped at the edge of a large parking lot. They stared through the window.

At the far end of the lot, three cars were parked in front of an obviously vacant building. The paint on the building was peeling, and the landscape was overgrown with dry, yellow weeds. A faded For Lease sign dangled across the front entryway from a single corner bracket.

"Oh, wow," Kenny said as he peered beneath the sun visor. "They weren't kidding. What . . . a . . . shithole. I can see why the owner's planning to tear it down. He'd be doing it a favor."

Danny said, "Yup. Put it out of its misery."

"They really think they can turn it around and have this place ready for business in a week?"

"That's what they say." Danny bit his lower lip as he eyed the distressed building.

Kenny chuckled. "Can't wait to see that."

Danny stared for a second, then he shrugged and said, "They're supposed to be good at this. Let's go have a look."

A moment later, they dodged the dangling sign and were greeted by an argument taking place just inside. They entered and found Henry and Johnny and two other people hunched over a folding card table, staring at a set of blueprints. A fluorescent light flickered and buzzed ominously above them.

"It won't work, Henry," the lone female at the table said, shaking her head. She had a thick blaze of long auburn hair, tied back with a scarf. Danny recognized her as the young woman who'd been setting up cameras and equipment on Kate's movie set.

"Why not?"

"Simple—timing. Your timing's all messed up. I do set design for a living. I'm used to working fast, and I know what can be done and what cannot. What you're talking about here is just like building a set. It's what I do every day, and I'm telling you, what you're asking for cannot be done. I can get it done in a week, maybe less, that's for sure. But not what you're asking for here. Nobody can. Your wish list means two, maybe even three, weeks. We'd have to get permits to do it, and that alone could add a week or two, or maybe a month, depending on the city. Today's Tuesday. If you want to be open for business next Monday, which is what, the thirty-first? We gotta *move*, and that means we can't risk getting shut down because we made changes that needed permits. No permits."

Henry studied the plans. "What if we pushed back a week? Would that help?" He looked up at Danny and lifted an eyebrow.

"Can't do it, Henry," Johnny said. "You got guys here from all over the world who gotta be back on time. Besides, unless I'm mistaken, this doesn't work for Danny either."

"Nope," Danny answered immediately. "It doesn't work for Kate—too much time means too much exposure and too much potential trouble. And doesn't work for Toni and me, as you well know. When the sixteenth rolls around, the rest of the world could be spinning backwards but I'd better damn sure be in church saying 'I do'." He shrugged. "Otherwise, I'll likely be dead, in which case it won't matter anyway."

"Point made," Henry said. "Doesn't work for anyone, then, does it?" He looked again at the plans, then said, "Okay, Murph. It's your baby. You have it ready for a walk-through by Sunday?"

She nodded. "Damn straight." She swept her arm over the drawings. "You don't need all this crap, anyway. We'll be ready. And it'll be great. You won't even notice the stuff that we leave out."

"Alright. Today's Tuesday. When do you think we can start moving equipment in?"

Murphy brushed back a strand of hair that had fallen across

her face as she turned to look at the dilapidated interior. "Well," she said after a moment's reflection, "time for the magic to happen. I'll call in some favors, and we can get a lot done in the next couple of days. Painting, flooring, lighting, glass—all that. I'll bring in some guys. We'll start right away, this afternoon. Kate cut me loose from the film for this—said I'm yours for the duration. So you get a hundred percent of my time. By Friday, I'll have your observation room and lab built, just the way you want. You can be moving furniture and equipment in by . . . let's say the weekend, Saturday. It'll be tight, but we'll get there. We'll work around the clock to make it happen. Come on, walk with me. I'll show you what I'm talking about."

* * * *

"Who was that?" Kenny said to Johnny after Murphy had left.

"Who was—?" Johnny glanced up at Kenny and saw where Kenny was looking. "Ohhh," he said. "You mean Murph? Well, sir," he said, slapping his hand on Kenny's shoulder, "that striking young bushy-haired maiden is known far and wide as Murphy Thompson."

"Murphy Thompson," Kenny repeated.

"That's right. She's the set designer for Kate Morgan's company. Kate loaned her to us for two weeks. Good thing, too, 'cause it looks like she's got some *mad* skills."

Kenny nodded slowly. "It would seem."

THE ROPERS

CHAPTER 13

Emerald Downs

"Your usual box, gentlemen?" The host smiled as he greeted Billy Thorne and Nigel at the entrance of the Turf Club at the Emerald Downs racetrack in Auburn.

It was Saturday afternoon, and the large room was beginning to get busy—the first race of the day was scheduled to start at two p.m., thirty minutes away.

"What's up, Carlos?" Billy said. "How ya doin'?"

"Excellent, Mr. Thorne, excellent." Carlos nodded toward the seats below. "We've got your normal booth reserved for you, of course. And they tell me there's an excellent card today. Hopefully, the afternoon will be *muy rentable* for you, no?"

Billy gave him a blank look.

"*Muy rentable*," Carlos explained. "Very profitable."

"Huh." Billy rolled his eyes as Nigel chuckled. "That'd

be different."

Carlos continued, unphased. "*Si*, I've got a good feeling for you today, Mr. Thorne. Many good things today. Here are today's racing forms." He handed each man a copy.

"Thanks." Billy turned and gazed through the panoramic windows. Ominous-looking low-hanging clouds drifted slowly from south to north. "How's the track?"

Carlos winced. "Aye, the track. Well, as you know, it rained last night—hard. I'm afraid the track—well, she's gonna be sloppy for sure."

Billy gave a quick smile. "Good. I like sloppy tracks. Poor bastards in the back look like they've been mud wrestling when they finish."

Carlos nodded, saying nothing. After a second, he added, "So, if you gentlemen are ready? I can take you now."

"Lead on."

From its entrance at the back, the Turf Club slopes downward like a movie theater to the towering wall of glass on the east side, where the stunning Cascade Mountains serve as a panoramic backdrop. The entire track was visible as Carlos led the men to their seats—starting gate, back stretch, even the distant barns beyond the far turn.

Carlos had nearly reached their table when Billy abruptly stopped. A woman was sitting alone, two booths removed from his reserved seats. She was lost in thought, leaning back in her seat and chewing intently on the end of a pen while she studied a racing form. The striking woman wore a wide gray hat with a sharply contrasting aqua ribbon over a sleeveless plain white sundress. Her hair was dark and shoulder-length, and her eyes were a deep azure blue. She had a stunning and colorful full-sleeve jungle tattoo on her left arm and a small Celtic weave on her right.

Billy stared for several moments until Nigel poked him, saying, "Uh, Billy?"

Trance broken, Billy beckoned to Carlos. "I think I'd like to change our seats today, Carlos," he whispered. "How about we sit at that one this afternoon?" He nodded discreetly toward the empty booth next to the woman.

Carlos looked at the woman, then he turned back to Billy and smiled. "Certainly, Mr. Thorne."

* * * *

Danny and Johnny stood inside the club, at the top of the room near the pari-mutuel betting machines. They appeared to be huddled in conversation, comparing racing tickets, absorbed in a heavy discussion about wagering. In reality, the two were looking past their tickets and carefully watching Billy as he approached Toni.

Johnny smiled when Billy stopped to change seats. "And that, my friend, is a fluttering bird."

"I get it."

"Soon as he saw her, he changed course like he ran smack into a wall."

Danny nodded. "I've seen it happen before."

"I'll bet. You're a lucky man, Logan."

"I know." Danny watched her for a moment, then he said, "She's nervous."

Johnny smiled. "She doesn't *look* nervous. She's ready."

"She practiced in front of the mirror last night."

"Like I said, she's ready. You're both ready. You'll be fine." He waited for a moment, then he fanned a stack of pari-mutuel tickets. "Your boy Kenny is a genius. You can't tell these aren't the real deal."

"I wouldn't try to cash one in. What happens if you get lucky and accidentally win?"

Johnny chuckled. "No sweat. Kenny made me two tickets for each race. At least one of them's guaranteed to be a loser. You have Toni's?"

Danny smiled. "Yep." He held out a large stack of tickets. "I just got to slip her the winning ticket at the end of each race. She's gonna look like the greatest horse picker the world's ever seen."

When Billy and Nigel were seated, Johnny said, "Okay—it's showtime."

They started down the path, and Johnny whispered, "And remember, from now on, we're in character." He gave a quick little bow. "Jimmy Albert, at your service."

* * * *

"I haven't seen you here before."

Toni glanced up from her racing form and looked at Billy

for a moment. "Well, maybe that's because I haven't been here before, at least not for a long, long time, anyway."

"Where've you been?"

"Away." She held up the racing form. "My dad used to bring me when I was little—a long time ago. I'm figuring out my bets."

Billy offered his hand. "I'm Billy Thorne."

"Toni Blair." She shook his hand and gave him an inviting smile.

"You here by yourself?" he said. "I could come over, give you a few pointers. Help out a beginner like yourself."

She smiled, but then she shook her head. "That's kind of you to offer, Mr. Thorne, but sorry, this is my fiancé."

Billy looked up to see Johnny and Danny approaching. His face dropped. "No problem." He turned back to his own booth.

"Oh, wait!" Toni said to Billy. "Danny, Jim, this is Billy Thorne and his friend . . ." She looked to the other side of the booth toward Nigel.

"Nigel," he said with a quick smile.

"And that's Nigel," Toni said, smiling.

Danny nodded, not smiling. "Nice to meet you." Then he slipped into the booth next to Toni and gave her a kiss on the cheek.

"You get it?" Toni asked Danny.

"I got it." He held up one of her tickets.

Toni smiled. "Excellent." She looked at Johnny. "And you?"

"I'm down, too," Johnny said. "Two thousand on a trifecta." He looked outside at the large tote board on the opposite side of the finish line. "C'mon, baby."

In the next booth, Billy immediately looked down at his racing form at the mention of the size of Johnny's bet. He stared hard for a moment, then he bent closer to the paper. He smiled and whispered something to Nigel, motioning backward toward Johnny with his head.

CHAPTER 14

Emerald Fusion Technology

At two p.m., Kenny Hale stepped into the middle of the wild and chaotic process of transforming Emerald Fusion Technology's "new" building in Bellevue. He stopped cold and stared, wide-eyed. Everywhere, people were busy—moving boxes, carrying equipment, touching up paint. The hectic comings and goings were punctuated by loud construction sounds emanating from deeper inside the building—hammering, sawing, drilling, and yelling. In just a few days, the dilapidated old building had been turned from a derelict shell into what appeared now to be a first-rate, high-tech laboratory/office, complete with new paint, a new outside sign, even new landscaping, right down to the dahlias planted at the front door. Someone had even scrawled EFT World Headquarters on a piece of cardboard and taped the sign to one of the lobby walls.

He was admiring the work when a gruff voice behind him

said, "Excuse me there, buddy!"

Kenny turned and saw that he was about to be run over by a man carrying a large box. He quickly stepped out of his path as the man lumbered by.

"Say, man," said a man in a white lab coat standing in the doorway.

Kenny turned, but before he could say a word, the man asked, "Where we supposed to be?"

Kenny looked around for a moment, making sure he was the one being addressed. He pointed a finger at himself. "You're asking me? I'm not sure. I'm just here to set up—"

"You an extra?"

Kenny turned and was surprised to see that Murphy Thompson had entered the room, a well-worn tool belt strapped low on her hips. "No," he said, "I was just—"

"Not you," Murphy said to him. "I *know* who you are." She turned to the other man. "You. What do ya need?"

"I was told to report to Emerald Fusion Technology at two o'clock. Here I am."

"Lucky us." She scanned him up and down quickly. "You're an actor?"

The man nodded. "Yeah. Johnny Redmond told me to show up."

Murphy nodded. "All right. Down the hall there and hang a left through the second door. That's the lab. You'll see a good-lookin' silver-haired man named Henry Parker inside. Report to him. He's getting everything lined up for the run-through."

"Thanks."

Murphy watched, and when the man had left, she turned. "You're Kenny, right? From Danny's crew?"

Kenny nodded. "That's me. I'm here for the phones and the computers—some automation work."

Murphy glanced down at Kenny's electronics gear, bulging out of the case slung over his shoulder, then she looked back at him. "That you are." She smiled, then her eyes flew open wide. "Watch it!" she said, wrapping her arms around him and pulling him toward her as two workers labored under the weight of a large box, bumping the doorway as they went.

"Hey! You guys nick my walls, I'll have your asses!" she yelled over Kenny's shoulder. "We just did 'em, for Christ's sakes."

Murphy gripped him tightly. She had pulled him against her, and he now had her pinned against the wall. As soon as the crate had passed, Kenny stepped back.

"Sorry," he said. "I didn't mean to squish you."

Murphy laughed. "You didn't. This place is nuts today. Easy to get run over."

"Yeah, it is." He looked around. "This . . . progress is fantastic. You gonna be ready by tomorrow afternoon?"

She smiled. "Me? Finished on time? Hell yeah. I *never* miss a deadline. We're moving furniture and final equipment in right now. That's why all the traffic. Final clean's tonight. Henry's doing rehearsals now, and we're gonna do a final walk-through tomorrow. We'll be ready—you can count on it. I'm more worried about your programming, not to mention your boss and Toni and Johnny out at the track." She crossed her fingers. "If they don't come through, we got nothin'. All this is just a drill."

Kenny started to answer when two men entered the lobby, one with a clipboard and one rolling a hand truck loaded with equipment.

"Bellevue Audio," the man with the clipboard announced.

"Bellevue Audio," Murphy repeated. "You got my seat shakers?"

The man nodded. "Sure do. Where do you want 'em?"

"Duh. On the seats, of course. C'mon. Observation room. This way." Then she turned to Kenny. "You, too. After I get these guys situated, I'll show you around the world headquarters, and we can get started in the control room."

CHAPTER 15

The Trouble with Trifectas

"Damn!" Johnny said, watching the horses come across the line through his binoculars. "Fourth place! He was coming on strong! You see the way he closed? Horn something . . . Hornfel! I needed him to show. He had to swing wide around the final turn, but he was charging. What a horse! That was close! He just needed a longer race."

"Yeah," Danny agreed. "Maybe another mile or so. He practically fell down out of the gate."

"True. But he was comin'!" Johnny said. He turned to put the binoculars down as the trailing horses finished and brought the afternoon's fifth race to a close. "The two horse won, right? I was too busy watching Hornfel trying to catch up, and I didn't even—"

Johnny halted abruptly as he looked at Toni. She was leaning back in her seat, a huge grin on her face, holding up a winning ticket.

"Really?" Johnny said. "Are you kidding me? You won again? What's that? Three out of five?"

"Three out of three," she said. "I didn't bet the other two." She did a little shoulder-shift victory wiggle and held up three fingers. "I told you guys."

"Uh-oh, here she goes," Danny said.

"I've got a sys-tem . . . I've got a sys-tem," Toni chanted.

"You've got a system," Johnny said, shaking his head. "You've got a system, and I'm gettin' my ass handed to me on a plate."

Toni said gleefully, "Yep. My daddy showed it to me when I was just a girl. Still works."

"Care to share?" Billy Thorne said, turning in his seat. "Seein's how you're on a roll."

Toni stopped her victory dance. "Why, Mr. Thorne," she said, her eyes sparkling as she adopted a Southern accent, "you mean to say you could use the help of a . . . beginner like little ol' me?"

Billy stared at her but said nothing.

"Well . . ." Toni said with a smile. "Seeing's how we're such good friends and all, and I am in a good mood today, obviously, I'll let y'all in on my little secret."

Billy looked at her. "Do tell."

"Okay," Toni said, her voice reverting back to normal. "Place bets."

"'Scuse me?"

"Place bets," she repeated. "If the favorite is no better than three-to-one, I make a place bet on 'em. Good horse—decent payout. As long as he comes in first or second, I cash in!"

A slight scowl formed on Billy's face as he considered what Toni had said and considered the implications. "Place bets don't pay anything. You can't make any money with 'em."

"Sure you can," she answered. "I don't get rich quick, if that's what you mean. But slow and steady adds up. Besides, I'm three-for-three so I must be doing something right, right? I admit my system's not for a greedy person." She paused, a serious look on her face. "But you're not a greedy man, are you, Mr. Thorne?" she chided, her voice back to her Southern drawl.

"Hmph," Billy said.

Johnny rolled his eyes. "*I* damn sure am," he said. "And I'm getting nailed."

Billy shifted in his seat and turned to look at Johnny. "That's because *you're* bettin' exotics—exactas, trifectas, supers, right?"

Johnny nodded. "You noticed."

"How could I not, the way you've been crying over there? Here's a hint. Those are sucker bets, dude—super-long odds. Hard enough to win at this game just picking one winner. With your bets, you gotta pick 'em all—and you gotta pick 'em in order."

Johnny nodded. "Yeah, but the payoffs are great. I hit one ticket, and I'm golden."

"Yeah, and till then, you get crushed," Billy said. "You were bettin' two large per race? Five races so far today? You're down ten grand? And the day's just half done?"

Johnny shrugged but didn't answer.

"Damn, dude. What's the big hurry, you don't mind my askin'? What's so important you gotta just throw your money away?"

Johnny took a quick breath. "I got a chance to . . . I can't use Toni's method—slow and steady. I don't have that kind of time." He grimaced. "I need a big score." He stood and looked out over the track for a moment, then he said, "Toni, you want to walk up to the machines with me, lay down our bets for the sixth?" He turned slightly and quickly winked at Danny.

* * * *

Johnny and Toni were still at the pari-mutuel machines, leaving Danny alone at the booth. He was pretending to study the *Racing News* when Billy turned around.

"Your buddy ain't doin' so well, is he?"

Danny rolled his eyes. "That's the truth."

"Why's he in such a hurry to lose his ass like this?"

Danny glanced up at the top of the room, then turned back to Billy. "I shouldn't say, but between you and me, the company Jimmy works for is getting sold in a week. He's got an option to buy in before the sale, but it's the kind where he has to come up with the cash by then—else he's out. Time's runnin' short, so . . . he's down to betting longshots."

"Doesn't appear to be paying off for him," Billy said.

"No, it does not."

After a moment, Billy said, "I gotta ask. What's his deal, anyway? He's willing to lose that kind of dough, what's the payoff? What happens if a lightning bolt hits, and he suddenly gets lucky?"

Danny glanced back up towards the betting machines, then, his voice lowered, he said, "Then he gets to turn a two-million-dollar buy-in into a twenty-million-dollar profit in a week."

Billy's eyes widened. "Whoa! Twenty million bucks! The hell kind of company is it, anyway? Some kind of internet deal? They come up with some new way to sell diapers online? Something like that?"

"Nope." Danny looked around to make sure no one else was listening. "Better. Energy—clean energy."

"Clean energy?" Billy said. "Like what? Solar?"

Danny shook his head. "No—they've invented a new kind of generator—a fusion generator. His company is called Emerald Fusion Technology. They've been working on this machine for, like, five years now. Sometime—about six months ago—they had some kind of breakthrough and the next thing you know, all the Wall Street money guys show up, just like that. People start waving around big bucks. Suddenly, after years, they all want in on the ground floor. Lucky for Jimmy, he has his buy-in option so he thought he was golden—all set. The plan was they were going to build the company up and then take it public. With his option shares, Jimmy thought he was going to be a billionaire."

"Thought?"

"Yeah. Then Jimmy's boss, who also happens to own all the stock in the company, changed his mind. He decided he doesn't want to grow the company after all—doesn't want to wait that long. He's all done—no going public. Instead, he wants to cash out now, go play on a beach somewhere.

"So two weeks ago, he calls a meeting and announces that

the company's been sold—sold to a big Japanese company, Matsumoro Industries. No discussion, no nothing. Papers are signed, deal's done. Hundred million bucks. Good for him—bad for Jimmy. He stands to get screwed out of the chance to become wealthy unless he can pony up by next Saturday. Danny shook his head. "I feel for the guy. His big shot's slippin' away, right in front of him. That's why he's getting a little desperate."

"A little desperate?" Billy asked. "How close is he? Do you know?"

Danny shrugged. "Not that close. I think he has a 401(d) he can tap–maybe a 2nd mortgage. Probably four–five hundred thousand total. Definitely not enough to make the deal. Which is the reason for today's Hail Mary."

"Yeah, I can see." Billy thought about it for a few seconds, then he gave a quick little chuckle.

"You see something funny in this?" Danny asked.

Billy shrugged. "Well . . . yeah. The poor bastard's got five more races to go to win a million and a half bucks. He's bettin' long shots and to top it off, he's a pretty crappy horse picker. He may as well be throwin' darts at the racing form. And one week left? There's no pressure, right? I'd say your boy's got his work cut out for him."

CHAPTER 16

Control Room

Kenny worked alone in what Murphy had set up as the control room in the back of the Emerald Fusion Technology shop. He was busy configuring a server with a large touchscreen, connecting relays, solenoids, and actuators, singing quietly to himself. He looked up and saw Henry Parker leaning in.

"You heard anything from your team?" Henry asked.

Kenny checked the time. "Not a word." He frowned. "I didn't know I was supposed to."

Henry shook his head. "Nah, you're not. I actually don't think we'll hear anything until they're in the car on the way home. I was just checking."

"Sorry."

Henry looked around at all the hardware. "How's it going in here, anyway? Takes a lot of gear, doesn't it?"

"Yeah, it does. But it's gonna be awesome. I took the time sheet you and Murphy put together, and I'm automating nearly everything. We'll be able to run the entire operation from this touchscreen, all wireless—every light, switch, bell, and valve. It's all going to work great."

"Good. Say, you know, I've been thinking. You know anything about cell phones?"

Kenny pushed his chair back from the desk. "Sure. Whatcha need?"

"I'm just thinking ahead. Is it possible to monitor a phone number so that when someone calls from a particular phone—or maybe a couple of different phones—instead of ringing the original number, the call can be intercepted and it can ring a different number instead?"

Kenny nodded. "Yeah, call routing. It's possible. It's not legal on someone else's number, though."

Henry smiled. "Neither is loan-sharking or stealing someone's painting."

"True." Kenny stared at the phone again, then looked up at Henry. "What do you need?"

* * * *

"I'd like to give a lab tech position a shot."

Henry and Lulu were seated behind Henry's desk at Emerald Fusion Tech, interviewing actors for the few remaining roles. A tall, gruff-looking, middle-aged man stood across the desk from the two. His hands were as big as both of Lulu's put together.

She flipped through a binder on the desk. "I don't think we need any more lab techs, Luther."

Luther looked at her, his face tight. "You mean I don't fit the part?"

Lulu looked up at him. "I mean I have all the slots filled, Luther. And besides, even if I didn't, I wouldn't bullshit you—I'd tell you." She looked down and flipped through Henry's notes. "Let me see what we've got here." She continued turning pages until she reached the end. She looked up and said, "I don't—"

"We're short a security guard."

Lulu looked up as Henry leaned in. "We are? I didn't know we even needed—"

"You won't see it on the page 'cause I forgot to list it," Henry said. "I've been meaning to add it." He turned to Luther. "What do ya think, Luther? You do a security guard?"

Luther laughed. "Bank guard . . . office guard . . . prison guard, even . . . Lord knows I seen plenty of 'em in my day. What do ya want? Tough guy? Mother Teresa?"

Henry smiled. "Let's see . . . I got it! You're Lamar Cole, head of security. You won't be bustin' any heads. You'll just be standin' around directing traffic, saying, 'Yes, sir' and 'No, sir.'"

Luther chuckled. "I'm used to that, too." He gazed at the ceiling. "Lamar Cole, head of security." He smiled. "Got a ring to it, don't it? Do you want me armed or unarmed? You know, I'm not supposed to have a firearm."

"Noooo," Henry answered quickly. "Unarmed. *Definitely* unarmed."

"Good. Do I need my own uniform?"

Henry shook his head. "Nope. No weapons, and we'll rustle up an extra-large Emerald Fusion uniform for you."

"I'll take care of it," Lulu said. "Somewhere. I'll have one by tomorrow for the final run-through, though."

Luther smiled, and tears began to well in his eyes. "Lulu, Mr. Parker, I can't tell you what this means to me. I appreciate the opportunity. You always been good to me, and I'm happy to be working with you again. This'll make the third time since I got out in 2000. I'm glad to have the work. And especially for the chance to help you out with that son of a bitch Frank Thorne."

Henry stood and extended his hand. "It's my pleasure. Sorry we haven't been around these parts much. But it's good to have you back. Tomorrow at one o'clock for the run-through."

When Luther was gone, Lulu said, "You just invented that. We don't need any security guards."

Henry shrugged. "Luther's a good man. We can make room." He stared at the door for a moment, then he looked down at his watch.

CHAPTER 17

The Rope

"How well you know this guy, anyway?" Billy said, looking up toward the betting machines. Toni and Johnny had just started making their way back down to the booth. "You sound like you're convinced this machine they've got is real."

"That's because it *is* real—we've seen it–Toni and I both. We've seen it work with our own eyes. Emerald Fusion hired my agency to run some background checks on a few of their key employees. We've gotten to know them pretty well. We've been there maybe three times in the past six months when they did test runs. Each run was awesome."

"You're in security?"

"Sort of. We own a private investigation agency over on Lake Union called Logan Private Investigations."

Billy chuckled. "Is that right?"

"Yeah. What's so funny?"

"You happen to know a PI named Farley Palmer?"

"Palmer . . . Palmer." Danny scrunched up his forehead and stared off into the distance. "I think I've heard the name, but I don't know him. Why? Should I?"

"Nah, he's just another PI. I figured you guys might know each other."

Danny laughed. "There's like two thousand PIs in Washington. Don't know 'em all."

"Makes sense. So you saw it run, this machine of theirs?"

"Yeah, we did. It's damn impressive."

Billy shrugged. "Then again," he said, "you're a PI. What do you know about this kind of stuff?"

"Fair question," Danny said. "And the answer is, I don't know a thing about chemical energy generation and all that technical crap. But, my God! They fire it up, and that machine gets goin', and the ground starts shaking—literally! It's gotta be the real deal. No wonder the hedge fund jumped in so fast."

"What hedge fund?"

"James Street something-or-other hedge fund. They're the ones putting up the money for building the full-scale working prototype for the Japanese these guys are working on. Something like four million dollars. *I* may not know anything about the science, but *they* sure do. This stuff's their *business*. They're in it every day, and they're in big. Makes me wish I had two million bucks to go in with Jimmy. I could probably cut myself in on a helluva deal."

Billy smiled. "Yeah, then again maybe your friend finally

gets lucky this afternoon, doesn't need ya."

"Maybe. But—"

"But it ain't lookin' good."

"No, it's not," Danny conceded. "Twenty million bucks slippin' past . . . you gotta feel for the guy."

Billy shrugged. "Not meanin' for anyone to read anything into this, but if there really was an opportunity to help your buddy cash in on his option, how could a guy get a look at this machine first? Before the Japanese show up?"

"They're pretty hush-hush about it, but I know they're planning on running another test or two next week before the Japanese get here on Saturday. Jimmy could probably get you a seat at one of those. If you're interested, why don't you ask him? Won't cost you anything to come and see it run."

Billy said nothing.

A few moments later, Johnny and Toni returned to the table.

"Hey, Jimmy," Danny said, "when's your next test run?"

"Monday," Johnny answered. "We're checking grid saturation. And James Street is going to be in town anyway, so they're stopping by, too. Why?"

Danny nodded toward Billy. "You might have someone here who wants to see it run."

Johnny turned to Billy. "Really? You wanna come see LEO run?"

"LEO?" Billy said.

"Yeah, that's the name we gave our machine. LEONARDO. LEO, for short. You interested in having a look?"

Billy answered slowly. "Maybe. Maybe not. But if we do,

when and where?"

"Monday morning, ten a.m." Johnny handed him a business card. "Our address is on my card."

Billy stared at it for a moment, then he looked up. "Ten o'clock, huh?"

"That's right."

Billy shrugged. "If I'm not there by a quarter after ten, it means I'm not comin'. So don't wait for me."

CHAPTER 18

Trail Runner

Sunday morning late, Billy was at the pool, relaxing in a lounger, working on a michelada, lost in thought. His straw hat was pulled low over his eyes, and he was staring at a picture of *Lilies* on his phone when he noticed a shadow move across the lounger. With one finger, he poked the hat up a little and saw the silhouette of someone standing next to him.

"Excuse me, Mr. Thorne. I hope I'm not bothering you."

Billy turned the screen off, then sat up. He shielded his eyes from the bright sunlight and saw Farley Palmer standing before him, a folder in his hand.

"Palmer," Billy said, sitting up straight. "On a Sunday, no less."

Farley opened the folder and pulled out a sheet. "I wanted to drop this off with your father, but he doesn't seem to be at home. So I left a copy in an envelope with the maid, and I thought I should leave you a copy as well, given our conversation a few days ago."

Billy beckoned with his hand. "Let's see."

Farley handed him the paper. It was a printout of an email.

FROM: GERALD SMALLWOOD, FBI CRIME LAB, QUANTICO, VA
SUBJECT: SHOE PRINT ANALYSIS
Palmer, good to hear from you, buddy. I ran your casting, and the lab just got back to me with the following:
MFG: Salomon
MODEL: S/LAB SPEEDCROSS
SIZE: Men's 12
WIDTH: Standard
APPROX DATE OF MFG: 2019 to present

Palmer, basically, it's a high-end, trail-running shoe in size 12. The analyst said the shoe is still in production. They're expensive and not all that common, usually bought by serious runners and—most importantly—only carried by about a dozen specialty running stores in Seattle (see list attached). So there's your "in." Get busy "running" them down! Good hunting! BTW, you owe me a dinner!

Billy read the email again, then he looked up at Farley. "So, what's this mean?"

"It's good news. If the shoe would've been a Costco special, there might be millions of them out there. But the fact that it's a serious runner's shoe is very helpful. There won't be nearly so many of them. It's probably from a specialty store. I'll just start calling the stores on the list and see if I can shake something loose. Who knows?" He turned to leave.

"Hey!" Billy called out. "Wait a second." He reached for his wallet and rummaged through it for a moment before pulling out a business card. "You know a PI named Danny Logan? Logan Private Investigations? Says his office is on Lake Union."

Farley nodded. "I've heard of him. He runs a small firm. Used to be owned by a partner of mine."

"Good reputation?"

"Far as I know. Mind if I ask why you're asking?"

Billy said nothing for a moment, then he said, "No. Nothin' important. Nothin' to do with any of this stuff you're workin' on."

THE TALE

CHAPTER 19

Test Drive

Danny pulled out his phone and glanced at the time. 10:01 on a sunny Monday morning, the last day of August.

"Where is he?" Toni asked, looking out the Emerald Fusion Technology front door.

"He'll be here," Johnny said. "We set it up well. He'll be here."

"Where's your guy? Is he coming?" Danny turned and saw Murphy walking toward him.

"He hasn't left yet. Doc's watching the house. He's gonna call when he leaves."

"Chill, guys," Johnny said. "The mark always makes you wait—it's part of their deal. They want to show everyone who's boss."

"Geez, I hope that's what it is," Murphy said as she looked around. "Otherwise, we went through a crapload of trouble for nothing."

Johnny smiled. "Just watch."

"Well, my fingers are crossed. We're ready—we're all set up inside."

"Good. When he gets—"

He was interrupted by Danny's phone, beeping to indicate a new text.

Murphy jumped. Danny pulled out his phone and looked at the text from Doc. *BT moving. Headed East on 24th. ETA 10–15 minutes.*

"You were right," he said. "He's headed our way."

* * * *

Ten minutes later, Murphy called out, "They're driving up! Round one! Just like yesterday! Places, everyone!"

When everyone was ready, she turned to Johnny. "Okay?"

He smiled. "Send it."

She turned and yelled, "Action!"

Murphy spun away and marched off to the control room as the building sprang to life. Men and women in suits suddenly appeared, walking beside white-coated scientists, deep in conversation. Other lab technicians hustled back and forth between the office section of the building and the newly constructed "lab." Luther Rawlins, dressed in a crisply pressed security uniform, was seated at the front desk near the door.

Murphy walked into the control room as Kenny tapped a

command into his computer. Immediately, the telephone switchboard started ringing. Computers, gauges, and lights in the office and in the lab began blinking.

The office had been built so that two doors led directly off the lobby—one to the lab and one to the observation room. In addition, a long corridor led to the back of the building where more offices were located. A large window had been built into the wall between the lab and the observation room, allowing visitors to sit in comfortable theater-style chairs and watch what was happening in the lab.

Inside the lab itself, a clear plexiglass cylinder the size of a fifty-five-gallon drum was perched on end on a stout stainless-steel platform in the center of the room. Bright green letters painted on the cylinder read LEONARDO 1.0. The cylinder was capped by a clear plastic dome, to which numerous hoses and cables were attached. LEONARDO was filled with an amber liquid in which a shiny metal tube was suspended vertically in the center. A steady stream of small bubbles slowly drifted upward from the bottom of the cylinder.

To one side of the lab, a large console of computer monitors was manned by four "technicians", who were busy carefully adjusting and studying the monitors, each displaying a variety of charts, graphics, and controls. Other technicians were busy checking fittings and gauges.

"Holy crap," Danny said to Toni. "I don't know what any of this is, but it looks good."

"It looks *really* good. I can't believe Murphy and Kenny pulled this together so fast."

"No wonder Kenny—"

"Here they come!" someone yelled through the doorway.

A short time later, Billy Thorne and Nigel walked in and stopped. Billy looked around, eyes wide, taking in the activity.

"Watch out, buddy!" a lab technician toting a large box said a few moments later as he hurried past.

Billy quickly stepped back. "What the hell . . . ?"

"Please step over this way, gentlemen," Luther called out, gesturing toward the security desk. "Out of the traffic pattern so you don't get run down. You two guests of somebody here?"

"Yeah, we're—"

"They're with me!" Johnny called out, emerging from the office corridor and walking across the lobby. He extended his hand. "Billy, Nigel, thanks for coming. Really. You're just in time."

Billy nodded, still looking around. "Place is a madhouse."

"Sure is. It's actually crazy this morning—even more so than normal. The hedge fund guys are here—I might be able to introduce you later. The Japanese will be here at the end of the week. So the boss wants to make a great impression for everyone. Plus, we started building the upscaled unit yesterday—LEONARDO 2.0—the full-sized reactor that the Japanese want to see on Saturday." He smiled and rubbed his hands together. "It's going to be awesome, a lot bigger. If you were looking for action, your timing is perfect." He lowered his voice. "I was able to get permission to have you sit in this morning." He turned to Luther. "Can you hook these gentlemen up with a couple of guest badges?"

Luther nodded. "Right away, sir."

"Why, Mr. Thorne," Toni said, smiling, as she and Danny

walked out of the office corridor. She held out her hand. "So nice to see you again."

Billy shook her hand. "You, too."

Billy's gaze was fixed on the propped-open door leading to the lab. The activity within was hectic. "That it?"

"It is. Meet LEONARDO." Johnny paused for effect. "Gentlemen, that right there is the keys to the friggin' kingdom."

Billy stared for a moment, then he said, "Is it ... uh ... ready?"

"Absolutely. The techs are running last-minute checks before this morning's test run."

Billy stared for a moment, then he turned back to Johnny. "You seem a little nervous."

Johnny lowered his voice to just over a whisper. "Hell yeah, I'm nervous. We're five days away from closing a hundred-million-dollar deal. Who wouldn't be nervous? It's not every day you get a chance to hit it big—really big—you know?" He nodded toward LEONARDO. "This right here is *my* chance. And if you have the means, I'm hoping *you'll* see the opportunity as well so you and I can work something out and get you in at the last minute before it's too late. After you see what LEO can do, that is."

"Hey, guys! What say we get this show on the road?"

They turned and saw that Henry and Buttons Greer had entered the lobby from the office section. Henry wore a white lab coat, while Buttons was sharply dressed in a crisp navy pinstripe suit and crimson power tie. A briefcase-toting, suited assistant trailed behind.

"Larry!" Johnny said, stepping over and greeting Buttons warmly. "Glad you could make it."

"Works out great," Buttons said. "We've got meetings here all week. We didn't want to miss the final test before the Japanese demo. Sorry we're a little late—the freeway from Boeing Field was murder."

"No problem, we're ready." Johnny put his hand on Billy's shoulder. "Hey, Billy! Let me introduce you. Meet Lawrence McElroy, better known in the industry as Larry M. Larry runs the James Street Global Energy Fund. They're a huge energy hedge fund out of New York City."

"Larry McElroy," Buttons said as he shook Billy's hand.

Billy gave a curt nod.

"And this fellow," Johnny continued, "is my boss, Myles Cohen."

Henry quickly shook hands with Billy, then he turned to Johnny. "Let's get rolling, shall we? Larry's running a tight schedule this morning. You got everything ready to go?"

Johnny nodded. "Sure do, boss."

"Good. So, come on this way, Larry," Lulu said, smiling. "You know the drill."

Lulu took Buttons by the arm and led him and his assistant through the door to the observation room while Henry entered the lab.

Billy stared at the men's backs as they left the lobby. "Pushy SOB, isn't he?" he muttered.

"Which one?" Johnny said.

"Take your pick."

Johnny chuckled. "Well, as to Myles, well, you're right, he is. As to Larry, he's a *rich* SOB, which is a little different. He's used to getting what he wants. His hedge fund's putting four million bucks into the company."

"Well, he's not the only one with—"

Lulu interrupted him when she stuck her head out of the observation room and smiled. "Toni, gentlemen, y'all coming? These guys are busy, ya know?"

CHAPTER 20

New World Record

"Just go ahead and take any of the empty seats," Lulu said, pointing to sixteen theater-style chairs arranged in two rows of eight seats, four to each side of a center aisle. The lights in the observation room were dim, causing the eye to be drawn to the brightly lit window at the front of the room where a wall of glass provided a panoramic view into the lab. Technicians scurried back and forth, working to prepare Leonardo for the test run.

Buttons, along with his assistant, took two front-row seats nearest the door. Billy and Nigel took front-row seats across the aisle from them, while Danny and Toni slipped into the back row.

"It smells like new construction in here," Toni whispered, her voice muffled by thick, dark blue carpeting and sound-absorbing fabric wall coverings. "And it sounds funny, too."

"They've insulated the walls," Danny said as he looked around.

A speaker was mounted above the window from which Danny could hear what appeared to be background sounds from an open mic in the lab. Henry was in the lab, talking to a group of technicians. Mounted above the speaker was a Radiation Warning sign, the red letters clearly visible even though the sign was not illuminated. A large gauge was mounted beside the sign, and three digital readouts were hung below the sign, all reading 0.0.

Johnny turned to Billy. "You guys all set?"

"Yeah. We're ready." He nodded toward the lab. "What are we gonna see? What's gonna happen?"

"Well," Johnny said, "you want the technical explanation or the short and sweet layman's explanation?"

"The one for people without a science degree."

"Fair enough." Johnny pointed to the window. "Meet Leonardo 1.0. The plexiglass cylinder you see in there with the dome on top? That's called the containment cylinder. That metal panel danglin' inside the cylinder is what we call the reaction grid. It's made out of a metal called palladium. That's where all the action takes place. That amber liquid surrounding the cylinder is called deuterium, more commonly known as heavy water."

Suddenly, the radiation warning sign at the front of the room flashed and a loud *beep* blared through the speaker.

Billy rose up from his seat. "What the hell?"

Johnny held his hands up. "Sorry about that. That's just a prerun test. The technicians are running through countdown procedures before we fire up. Nothing to worry about. I should've warned you."

Billy relaxed somewhat but continued to stare at the lab

with concern. "Is any of that crap in there radioactive?"

Johnny shook his head. "No, nothing like that." He paused. "Well, technically, there *will be* a reaction taking place, but it's a chemical reaction." He pointed to the technicians at the console. "See those technicians over there? In a minute, they're going to turn those big knobs, and that will start pulsing an electrical current to the grid on, then off, then on, then off again. Real fast, though—thousands of times per second. That'll cause that grid to start vibrating. When that happens, a reaction is going to occur. Ultimately, the hydrogen atoms in the grid will get turned loose, then they'll fuse up with the extra hydrogen molecules in the deuterium and make a whole new molecule—helium, in this case. You'll see a whole bunch of bubbles rising up—that's the helium. When that fusion happens, energy gets released—lots of energy, a lot more energy than what it took to get the process started in the first place. Matter of fact, if we do it right, there's a net gain of something like five or six times as much energy released as was applied to the grid in the first place. The energy takes the form of heat—heat that we'll be measuring. You can follow along with these three gauges up here." He pointed to the digital gauges below the Radiation Warning sign.

Billy stared, saying nothing.

Johnny continued. "People like our Japanese buyer want the technology because it's a pretty simple matter to channel all that heat and turn it into steam. Then they run the steam through a turbine of some sort. The turbine spins a generator, and out comes super-cheap, super-abundant electricity."

Billy furrowed his brow. "So you're saying this thing's basically a high-tech water heater? That's why we're here?"

"You could say that," Johnny said, chuckling. "But here's the good part, the part that's worth all the attention. LEO here, in his current 1.0 form, just as you see him, he can generate enough electricity to power a small village for, oh, about a thousand years."

Billy turned quickly. "Really?"

"That's right. Of course, someone would have to be around to refuel him then." Johnny laughed at his own joke.

"And no radiation?" Nigel asked, pointing toward the warning sign. "No danger?"

Johnny shook his head. "Nope. Radiation's not a problem. Like I said, most of the energy gets released as heat, not radiation."

"Most?"

"Yeah, most," Johnny soothed. "Technically, once the fusion process gets going, there is a teeny-weeny, *small* release of gamma radiation, but it all gets contained within the reaction cylinder. We monitor it, as well."

Lulu nodded. "As long as we keep the reaction inside the cylinder there, we're good. Besides," she said, flashing Billy a wide smile, "you look like you're in pretty good shape. If you hear alarm bells and see the warning lights go on, just jump on up and run like hell."

Billy blinked.

Johnny feigned horror, then he laughed. "Will you please stop terrorizing our investors?" He turned to Billy. "She's joking with you. Pay her no mind at all. She's been doing this too long, and she has an evil little sense of humor."

Billy stared at her, his face serious.

Lulu laughed. "Relax, boys. We haven't lost anyone . . . yet."

"We've seen it twice now," Buttons volunteered. "It's pretty amazing."

"You guys about ready in there?" Henry addressed the room from the lab, his voice coming through the speaker at the front of the room.

"We're ready to go. I'll be in in a second." Johnny turned to the group. "If you all will excuse me, I'm needed in the lab for the test." He turned to Billy and lowered his voice. "Don't leave until I catch up with you when we're done, okay?"

He exited the observation room, and a moment later, Danny saw him enter the lab.

"Okay, guys," Lulu said from the front of the room. "We're all set. Kick the tires and light the fires!"

* * * *

Henry nodded to one of the lab technicians, who entered a string of commands into her keyboard. At first, nothing appeared to happen. Then, suddenly, the lights in both the lab and the observation room flickered, then came back on strongly. The monitoring gauges above the window at the front of the observation room sprang to life, while the lab began buzzing with activity. A steady stream of voices could be heard through the speaker—Henry issuing orders, others calling out numbers and gauge readings.

"Here we go!" Lulu said as she rubbed her hands together.

"Watch the three monitor gauges. This readout here on the right is the ratio between power in and power out—we call it the coefficient of power, or COP, for short. The COP is the key—the higher, the better. We're shooting for 5.0 today—five times as much energy coming out of LEO as going in."

"What's that one on top for?" Billy asked. "Next to the sign."

"That's the radiation level. It should stay at zero."

Billy stared, a worried look on his face.

The bubbling inside LEO suddenly increased, and Danny heard one of the lab technicians call out, "Pressure is fifty-two psi, Myles."

"Good," Henry answered.

"They're talking about pressure in the containment cylinder," Lulu said. "At fifty-two psi, it's just a little higher than a car tire and a little less than a bicycle tire. Our containment cylinder is super heavy duty, specially designed to withstand five hundred psi, about the same as a nuclear submarine at one thousand feet or so. It won't even notice fifty-two."

A moment later, she called out, "Okay! Look now, you can see that the COP's at 2.5 and coming up—more than twice as much energy coming out as going in. Which means we've got fusion!"

"Input power to seventy-five percent," Myles said, his voice clear through the speaker. The lab technicians turned to look at him.

"Seventy-five?" one of them asked.

Henry nodded. "Seventy-five."

"It'll show up on the grid," one of the techs protested.

"Not for long, it won't," Henry repeated. "Just do it."

Billy stared at Henry, then he turned to Lulu.

Lulu spoke carefully. "We try to avoid . . . regulatory entanglements by staying under the radar. We're planning on using off-grid generators for the big demo on Saturday with the Japanese, but the generators aren't here yet, so for now, our input power comes from the local power grid. When we crank up the input current, we run the risk of the technicians at the power company noticing the spike. Then they report it to the wrong people."

"Why? Is it illegal?"

"No, not strictly speaking. But it can lead to bureaucratic red tape we'd just as soon avoid. We'd have to explain the spike to some people we'd rather not have to talk to. We're just trying to stay off the charts for the next week. Or at least we were." She glanced at the window. "Sometimes, the boss has to show off. That's why they're reminding him."

Just then, the COP gauge jumped up to a reading of 4.8.

"Wow," Lulu said. "That's almost a new record." The gauge kept rising.

When the gauge rose past 5.0 a few seconds later, Lulu called out, "That's it! A new Emerald Fusion Technology record!"

Suddenly, the floor beneath the chairs began to rumble, faintly at first, then more pronounced. The glass window began to vibrate.

Billy jumped up. "What the hell?" Almost immediately, he turned and looked at the Radiation Warning sign, as if he expected it to be going off. However, the radiation gauge continued to read 0.0. The sign was quiet.

"It's okay," Lulu said. "LEO is reinforced and bolted to the concrete slab for support. Sometimes he starts to resonate at these high outputs. Don't worry, it's normal."

Billy sat back down, but he gripped the chair tightly. Meanwhile, the COP continued to rise, and the floor continued to rumble off and on until two minutes later when Henry called out, "That's it, boys and girls! Shut it down!"

* * * *

After the experiment had ended, an impromptu victory celebration was in full swing in the Emerald Fusion Technology lobby. Champagne flowed freely, despite it barely being noon. "5.4!" Henry high-fived Buttons. "A new high!"

Buttons nodded, smiling broadly. "That son-of-a-bitchin' floor started shaking, and I thought, 'Uh-oh! Here we go again.' But you didn't blow us to smithereens this time."

Henry chuckled, a champagne flute in his hand. "I didn't blow you to smithereens last time either. We blew the top off the containment cylinder, as you'll recall. One little incident six months ago, and you act like it's gonna happen every time. What'd I tell you, huh? The new cylinder is ten times as strong. It'll hold."

"Well, I'm glad of it. Congratulations! You deserve it!"

"Me?" Henry said. "*We* deserve it. And come next week, by God, we're finally going to collect. I tell you, every time we refine the grid, we get better results. We preloaded it with hydrogen for three days this time, and look at the result."

At that moment, Johnny, who'd been waiting with Billy Thorne, interrupted Henry.

"Say, boss, I was wondering if you still had a minute to talk to Billy and me?"

Henry stopped and turned to Johnny. He glared at him. "You *can* see that I'm right in the middle of an important conversation here, right?"

"Yeah. It's just that I wanted to make sure and—"

Henry held up his hand, and Johnny stopped talking immediately. His mouth opened, but no sound came out. "You guys just have a seat over there, and when Mr. McElroy and I get finished talking, we'll talk." He turned to Buttons. "Larry, let's head on back to my office, shall we? Get a little privacy. I want to talk something over with you."

After the two men rounded the corner down the hall, Billy Thorne turned to Johnny.

"Your boss is a bit of a jerk, you know?" Billy said as they watched the two men round the corner and walk down the hall.

"The thought occurs to me on a fairly regular basis," Johnny agreed.

"And he can't hold his liquor very well either."

"True, again."

* * * *

Billy jumped up. "To hell with this," he said to Johnny. "It's been ten minutes. I'm tired of waitin'." He turned to Nigel. "We're outta here."

At that moment, Henry and Buttons reentered the lobby, Lulu trailing behind.

"So, we're good then, right?" Buttons said, an air of command in his voice. "We stay the course?"

Henry nodded. "You bet. We're golden. Five days to go."

"Right on," Buttons said. "See you on Saturday. Be sure and let us know if you run another test this week. If we can get away from the meetings, we'd like to stop by."

After Buttons left, Henry sighed deeply, then he turned to Billy and Johnny. His eyes narrowed. "All right. You guys are up. Five minutes."

"Right here?" Johnny asked.

"Yep. Right here. And I know what you want. Let me start out by saying, I don't need any more money. Larry's group is coming in big-time. Four million bucks. We're all set."

"But you're not forgetting about my option, are you?"

Henry shook his head. "No, I'm not forgetting. Why? What happened? The racetrack pay off? You suddenly got two million bucks?"

"Well . . ." Johnny stuttered.

"I do."

Johnny and Henry both turned.

Billy looked at Johnny, then back at Henry. "I'm backing him. And I've got two million bucks."

"*You've* got two million dollars?" Henry said.

Billy nodded. "Yep."

"Liquid?"

Billy wavered, "Well, not exactly."

"Not exactly," Henry sneered. "What the hell's that mean, 'not exactly'?"

"It means," Billy said, "that I've got an oil painting, a very valuable oil painting. It's worth a damn sight more than two million. I'll put the painting up. You sell it, keep the difference."

Danny gave a barely noticeable victory clenched fist, but his hands remained at his sides, and his face betrayed no emotion.

Henry scoffed. "An oil painting? The hell am I gonna do with an oil painting? I need a new palladium lattice screen grid, and I need it by the end of the week." He waved his arm toward the lab. "I need four hundred gallons of deuterium. I sure as hell can't turn a damn painting into a palladium grid." He shook his head and looked at Johnny. "What are you trying to pull?"

"Hey, buddy, listen," Billy said. "This ain't just any painting. It's a classic. It's worth two million, easy, probably more. You're getting it at a bargain."

Henry shook his head again. "No, you listen, pal. I don't give a rat's rear end if it's the *Mona* friggin' *Lisa* and it's the bargain of the century. I got *no* use for an oil painting. That ain't gonna happen."

"Wait a second," Danny said. "I've got an idea."

Henry looked at Danny. "Logan?" he said.

"Toni and I know someone who owns a gallery downtown. The gallery has high-end clients. We did a job for them a while ago. They buy art all the time. They might know a collector, someone who might be interested. All it takes is a call. Then, if they do have a buyer, you'd have your cash." He turned to Billy. "That work for you?"

Billy shrugged. "Yeah. But remember it's two million bucks—not a penny less."

"I know." Danny turned to Henry. "And you?"

Henry pretended to mull over the idea, saying nothing.

"Don't forget," Johnny said. "We have a deal."

After a moment, Henry nodded. "All right. It'll cost me big-time, but I'll honor my end. Your option says two million cash for twenty percent, good until the company's sold. You got five days. I don't care where you get the money, as long as it's cash by Saturday before Matsumoro gets here." He glanced at Billy. "No oil painting."

Danny nodded. "Okay. Let me give her a call."

* * * *

Ten minutes later, Danny returned to the lobby. "I have good news," he said. He turned to Billy. "I spoke to our contact at the art gallery. I told her about your painting. You're right, it really is a high-value item."

"Told ya."

Danny nodded. "The gallery made a call to an interested party while I was on the line, a collector named Ricardo Velazquez. He knows the painting, missed out on buying it three years ago. Says he's absolutely a buyer now—he wants it for two million. Anyone ever hear of him?"

No one said anything, so Danny continued. "They told me he owns a life insurance company somewhere. Got tons of money."

"How fast can he move?" Henry asked. "We're down to a matter of days here."

"The gallery said he could close by the end of this week, no problem." Danny said. "But they also said that they want to get an appraisal on the painting first. They want to bring in their own expert."

"Appraise all you want. Price is firm," Billy said.

"I don't think the appraisal is to determine value," Danny said. "She sounded like it was just to make sure the painting is real."

Henry turned to Billy. "Your painting on the up-and-up, Thorne?"

Billy gave him a quick, dirty look before turning back to Danny. "When do they want to do this appraisal?"

"She mentioned tomorrow or Wednesday. They have to schedule their appraiser."

Johnny turned to Henry. "Boss?"

Henry stared at him for a moment, then he shrugged. "Like I said, long as I have the cash before the Japanese get here, I'll hold up my end of the deal."

* * * *

Danny and Johnny accompanied Billy and Nigel to their car in the parking lot. "Appraiser day after tomorrow, one o'clock?" Danny asked, looking up from his cell phone. "That work for you?"

Billy said agreeably, "Yeah, it works."

Danny shifted back to his phone. "We're on. I'll text you the address. Thanks."

Johnny rubbed his hands together. "So, there you go. We'll split my option fifty-fifty, just like we talked about. We're gonna make a boatload of money, partner. Ten million bucks apiece." He paused, suddenly concerned. "Is there anything else we need to do for you, you know, to make the deal happen? Anybody else we need to talk to?"

Billy sniffed. "Maybe. We'll most likely be talking to a few people, people who know more about this fusion stuff than I do, believe me."

Johnny nodded. "Good idea. You got anybody in mind?"

"Not yet."

"Most people won't have any idea what we're doing, but I got someone you could speak with," Johnny said as he reached into his pocket and pulled out his wallet.

"Who is it?" Billy said, raising an eyebrow. "A friend of yours?"

"Well . . . yes and no, actually." Johnny pulled out an old, worn business card. "Here, here's his card. If you want to talk to somebody who *really* knows this stuff, and you don't have anyone else, you can call my old university professor."

Billy took the card and looked at it for an instant.

Sean Flannery, PhD
Professor of Nuclear Theory
University of Washington

"Professor Sean was my advisor when I went through grad school. When it comes to physics, he's the real deal—a physics genius. If you need to talk to someone, you might start with him."

Billy eyed the card a moment longer, then he looked up. "All right." He turned to Danny. "So, appraisal on Wednesday. You both gonna be there?"

"*I'm* not," Johnny said. "I've got plenty to do around here getting ready for the Japanese demo. We're working hard on LEONARDO 2.0, the scaled-up version. Besides, I don't know squat about art. I'd just be in the way."

Danny nodded. "I don't know anything either, but our friend who owns the art gallery can't make it, and they want Toni and me to meet that Velazquez guy so he doesn't get nervous. So we'll be there."

* * * *

"You *are* going to get around to telling your old man what you've got goin', right?" Nigel said to Billy as they drove south on Lake Washington Boulevard. "I mean, selling the painting's one thing. Reinvesting the money's something else. He may have something to say about that, ya think?"

Billy took a quick breath. "I think he'll appreciate the return. But you're right, and I'll tell him. For now, though, all he needs to know is that we've got a buyer on the hook for two million, and the sale can close this weekend. Happens to be the honest truth. He'll like that. Naturally, the buyer wants an appraisal to make sure he's getting the real goods. He'll be okay with that, too. As to this little extra investment opportunity, I'll tell him about that after the appraisal."

Nigel glanced at him, then he turned back to the road.

CHAPTER 21

Trust but Verify

"Daaammn," Toni said as she and Danny drove down the long driveway from Hunts Point Road to the Thorne estate. She leaned forward and took in the imposing building ahead. "I knew it was nice in the dark, but in the daytime like this, the pictures don't do it justice. I'm half expecting to see footmen."

"And they say crime doesn't pay."

They rolled to a stop at the crown of the circular driveway. It was two minutes before one o'clock on Wednesday afternoon. They were just in time for the examination of the painting.

Toni continued to look around as they walked to the front door. "If you wanted, I wouldn't object to something like this for a wedding present."

Danny chuckled. "I'll add it to the list."

They were still admiring the home when the front

doors swung open.

"Good afternoon. Can I help you?" a housekeeper with a Southern accent asked.

"You may," Danny said. "We're here for the examination of the painting. I think we're expected."

"Okay. Y'all follow me, please. You're the first ones here."

They entered through heavy ten-foot-tall double doors and were immediately greeted by a wall of windows opposite them on the far side of a large living room. The windows perfectly framed a sweeping view across the sloping back lawn all the way down to Lake Washington and the city of Seattle beyond.

"Wow!" Toni said. "Nice!"

They followed the woman down a long marble-floored hallway until they entered another large room, this one with a view of the swimming pool. As soon as they entered, Danny abruptly stopped.

"Look at that," he said, nodding toward *Lys dans de Champs de Moret*, displayed on an easel in the corner of the room.

"Oh my," Toni said as she approached, her eyes sparkling. "That's spectacular. I don't believe I've ever seen anything quite like it before."

She examined the painting for a long moment, then she said, "I've been here, like, what? Two minutes? And already I can see why this Velazquez fellow is willing to pay a couple of million bucks for this thing. It's simply glorious. I wish *we* had the money."

"And a house on Hunts Point to put it in," Danny added.

"Right."

"So that means you like it, then?"

They turned to see that Billy Thorne had entered the room, along with Nigel.

Toni gave them a wide smile. "Hiya, Billy." She turned back to the painting. "And yes, I do like it—you did well. It's amazing. How'd you ever come by it, if you don't mind my asking?"

Billy shrugged as he walked over. "I don't mind. It actually found us. Thorne Financial's business is specialty finance. We make large loans to people, and sometimes we collateralize the loan with property like this painting here. Every so often, things don't work the way they're s'posed to, and we end keepin' the collateral as repayment." He nodded toward the painting. "That's what happened here."

"Well," Danny said, shaking his head, "I suppose someone's loss will be Ricardo Velazquez's gain."

The doorbell rang, and the housekeeper left. She returned a few moments later, accompanied by Sal DeVito, impeccably dressed in a charcoal suit with a yellow-and-silver-striped tie. "Good afternoon. I'm Ricardo Velazquez. And this gentleman"— he stepped aside—"is my appraiser, Dr. Simon Kristofferson."

A heavily made-up Kenny Hale stepped forward. "Ladies and gentlemen," he said with a flourish, "it's my pleasure."

Toni suppressed a laugh, covering her mouth and pretending to cough. Murphy and Kate's theatrical makeup artists had completely transformed Kenny. A baby-faced thirty-year-old computer geek had become a sixty-year-old senior citizen in the course of a couple of hours of work. Kenny's dark brown hair had been dyed black and then streaked with a generous dose of silver. Normally clean-shaven, he now sported a bushy salt-and-pepper mustache to match. His blue eyes had been rendered brown, courtesy of contact lenses. His relatively short demeanor had been augmented with very tall high-soled elevator shoes. The slight stoop that he had assumed gave the height back and made him seem much older.

"Whoa," Danny whispered.

"That's some makeup job," Toni agreed. "They showed me a picture of the real guy this morning. Kenny looks just like him."

"Ladies and gentlemen!" Kenny proclaimed in a surprisingly deep, gravelly voice, complete with a reasonable-sounding German accent. "Thank you for inviting me today!" He swept an arm across the vista. "And what a beautiful setting. Absolutely . . ." He paused when he saw the painting for the first time, then he continued. "Absolutely perfect as a backdrop for this magnificent work of art." He walked over to the painting. "So, here she is."

He stopped five feet away and gave a deep sigh as he admired the painting. A moment later, he turned to Sal and smiled.

"No one uses cadmium the way Sisley did," he said. "He used his own pigments. Brilliant! That's why the dazzling orange lilies you see here seem to be jumping right off the canvas. Watch!" he said with a flourish as he pretended to catch a flower. He turned to Toni and handed it to her. "Mademoiselle."

Toni's eyes twinkled as Danny stifled a chuckle.

Sal seemed barely able to contain his excitement. "I've been waiting for a Sisley, but I never expected *Lilies* would become available."

"A truly fortuitous find," Kenny said. He turned to Billy.

"Shall we get started, then?"

"We've got one more coming. Give us a minute."

Danny glanced at Toni, and she shot him a look. One minute turned into two. "I'll bet Frank Thorne's coming," he whispered. "It would be just like him to make us wait."

Toni looked at him, a trace of surprise in her eyes.

Three more minutes passed, and Danny whispered to Toni, "Screw this. I'm gonna take a look around while we wait."

Her eyes opened wide. "What?"

"Don't worry," he said. "Might come in handy to know the lay of the land around here, case we need to make a quick getaway. I'll be right back." He turned to Billy. "While we're waiting, can you point me to the restroom?"

"Through that doorway, turn left and down the hall," he said. "It's the second door on your right."

* * * *

A few minutes later, Danny opened the restroom door, looked both ways, and saw that the hallway was empty. In the great room, he could hear Kenny explaining an art technique to Toni. Danny stepped out and began to walk slowly down the hall in the opposite direction, away from the great room.

He scouted the home as he went. Artwork adorned the walls, but nothing like the Sisley sitting on the easel in the great room. Even to Danny's untrained eye, the pictures on the walls were obviously poster prints, the type of art one might find in an inexpensive hotel room.

Suddenly, a girl popped out of a side room with her head down and nearly bumped into him.

"Oh!" she said. "Excuse me, I—" She stepped back and fell silent.

"Sorry," Danny said. "Are you okay?"

Then Danny also froze as he recognized her. Chloe.

She smiled, looking up at him. "I'm the one who's sorry. I . . . you look *really* familiar. Do I know you?"

Danny smiled. "I'll bet you say that to all the strange guys wandering around here who are lost, don't you?"

Chloe giggled and shook her head. "We don't get many of those." She stared at him intently for a few moments. "I swear I've seen you somewhere before, but I'm damned if I can figure out where."

Danny smiled. "What's your name?"

"Chloe. Chloe Rogers. I work with Mr. Thorne. Uh, Billy Thorne, that is."

"Chloe . . ." Danny said, looking up and rubbing his chin. "Chloe . . . You didn't happen to go to the University of Washington, did you? Criminal Justice Department?"

She giggled again. "College?"

Danny smiled. "Yeah, U-Dub. Criminal Justice Department."

She gave a quick laugh and was about to answer when a door across the hall opened. Doyle Reese stepped out, followed by Farley Palmer.

Chloe looked at the two men and quickly said, "Excuse me." She spun around and left.

Danny watched her go, then he turned to the men. "Sorry, I'm here for the painting appraisal. Had to use the restroom, and I got turned around—went the wrong way back. She was pointing me back to civilization."

"It happens," said Doyle. "You are?"

"Danny Logan."

"Mr. Logan, I'm Doyle Reese. I work with Mr. Thorne. Frank Thorne, that is." He nodded toward Farley. "This is Farley Palmer."

"Farley Palmer . . ." Danny said. "I've seen your name. You're a PI, right?"

Farley nodded. "I am. And I've seen your name as well. I understand you took over my old partner Richard Taylor's practice when he retired."

"That's right." Danny extended his hand. "Good to meet you, Farley."

Farley reached for Danny's hand. "And you. How is Rich—" He stopped, his eyes lowered. He froze for a moment, then he looked up. "Say, those are nice shoes! Are those . . ."

"Salomons," Danny said. "Speedcross trail runners. I love 'em. Are you a runner?"

"Me?" Farley smiled. "Oh, no, I just—"

"Danny!" Toni had stepped into the hall behind him from the great room. She gestured to him. "They're about to get started with the examination in here."

"Okay, good." Danny turned back to the men. "Gentlemen, my meeting. I've got to scoot. Nice meeting you both."

"I'll be joining you shortly," Doyle said.

Farley smiled. "Say 'hello' to Richard for me, will ya?"

"You bet." He walked back down the hall to Toni. When he reached her, she whispered, "Having fun?"

"See who that was?"

"I did. And *you'll* never guess who's about to join us."

"Frank Thorne, right? He just finished his meeting."

"Nope."

Danny glanced at her as they continued walking. "Who?"

"I just found out that the Thornes are bringing in their *own* art expert. They want someone to verify the good Dr. Kristofferson's findings. They're supposed to be here any minute now."

CHAPTER 22

The Real Deal

"Be ready to bail if it goes bad," Danny whispered as he and Toni made their way back to the great room. "If it blows up, you get Kenny. I'll grab Sal." They rounded the corner into the great room.

"Billy's gone outside to fetch his art expert," Doyle said a minute later when he entered the room. Farley was no longer with him.

"Nope!" Billy said as he walked into the room from the front hallway. "We're here. She just got here."

He stepped to the side, and a dark-haired young woman followed him. She was dressed professionally in a business pantsuit and carried a briefcase. "This is Patricia Cole," Billy said.

"Call me Pattie."

Danny stared at her for a moment, then he turned to Billy. "Didn't know you were bringing your own expert. Mr.

Velazquez here could have saved the money he's spending on Dr. Kristofferson."

Billy shrugged. "Just a precaution."

"Excellent idea!" Kenny said in his gruff voice as he approached Pattie, smiling. "Two sets of eyes are better than one!" he said, extending his hand to her.

"Dr. Kristofferson, what an honor, sir." She shook his hand vigorously. "You're much younger than I expected."

Danny cringed, but Kenny just smiled. "The pleasure is all mine, my dear," he said in his gravelly voice. "My card." He handed her a business card. "You are an appraiser?" he asked. "Local?"

"No," she said, smiling.

"An authentication expert?"

She shook her head and smiled demurely. "Uh, no. I'm just a friend of Billy's. Actually, I'm a grad student at U-Dub in fine arts. I know a little bit, but nothing like you, of course. Billy asked me here to watch."

Danny glanced at Toni and raised his eyebrows. She gave a quick smile.

"But I took an authentication class, and we studied your methods," she said. "I was particularly impressed with the way you were able to uncover the Monet fraud."

Danny glanced at Kenny.

Kenny hesitated a moment, a puzzled look on his face. Then his eyes opened wide. "Oh! You refer to *The Seine at Port-Villez?*"

"Yes!" Pattie said, smiling. "That was great work on your part."

Kenny nodded. "I'd almost forgotten. Yes, unfortunate outcome for the museum, but a most satisfying assignment on a professional level." He turned to the group. "Ms. Cole is referring to an assignment I had in Germany several years ago. I was called in by the Wallraf-Richartz Museum in Cologne to authenticate a very expensive Monet. Almost immediately, I sensed something amiss. The signature was ... wrong, not Monet's, and upon examination under infrared light, it became clear that an aging coating had been applied to the work." He shook his head. "The work was quite obviously a forgery."

"Obvious to an expert like you, sir," Pattie said. "But as I recall, the museum was fooled. They displayed it for years before you exposed the forgery."

Kenny smiled modestly. "Just doing my job. I'm surprised you studied this in your class. I commend your professor."

"We—"

"Hey!" Billy interrupted, looking from one to the other. "I'm glad you're so impressed by each other. Now maybe we can get going here? I got places to be."

Danny beamed. He whispered in Toni's ear, "Round one to Kenny Hale."

* * * *

"So," Kenny said, pointing to a bound set of shipping documents he'd brought with him, "as you can clearly see by comparing the gallery exhibition labels affixed to the frame to the exhibition records in my reference documents, this painting completely matches what we would expect to see. Clear to everyone? Good.

Let's move on, then, shall we?"

His jacket had been removed, his tie loosened, and his sleeves rolled up.

Danny checked his phone. It was two fifteen. He took a deep breath and shook his head quickly.

"Wake up!" Toni hissed.

Danny nodded and looked around. Pattie Cole was wide awake, still paying rapt attention, as was Sal DeVito. Doyle Reese had excused himself and left the room ten minutes earlier. Billy paid no attention at all. Instead, he slowly used his thumbs to type a text message into his cell phone.

Screening himself from Billy, Danny caught Kenny's eye and made a circular wrap-it-up motion with his index finger. Kenny gave a nod.

"So, in summary—"

"Thank God," Billy muttered without looking up.

"In summary, let's review."

"Oh, geez." Billy shook his head and continued texting as Doyle returned.

Kenny continued. "*Lys dans de champs de Moret* is a well-known work of Alfred Sisley. There is absolutely no controversy or question as to attribution here. We know for a fact that Alfred Sisley created this masterpiece, and we know he did it in the summer of 1884. A pencil drawing of this picture appears near the beginning of a sketchbook that Sisley kept as a record of his work from November 1883 to summer 1885. An inscription on the drawing identifies the site as the field on the road from Moret to Saint-Mammès, which runs along the Loing river. Sisley established himself in this area, on the edge of the Forest of Fontainebleau, in 1880, and was captivated by its 'quite picturesque views,' as he put it at the time." He looked up and smiled. "I love how he says that. In fact, he settled permanently in Moret in 1889. With the attribution resolved, the remaining question, then, becomes one of authentication—or, is the painting real?

"For that, we first examine the artist's style and hand, what we call in my business . . ." He paused and looked at Pattie Cole. "Ms. Cole?"

"Morellian analysis?" she answered shyly.

Kenny beamed. "Precisely! Morellian analysis. And this painting passes all the tests with flying colors!"

"Kenny knows less than I do about art," Danny whispered to Toni. "How's he remember all this?"

Toni shrugged. "Good coaching."

"So what's all this mean?" Billy said. "Are we okay here?"

Kenny nodded. He turned to Sal. "What it means, Mr. Velazquez, is that you are a very lucky man. You've found a real treasure here."

Billy smirked. "Just like I said."

THE SHUTOUT

CHAPTER 23

The Professor

The deep blue of the late afternoon sky was punctuated by lazy, billowing cumulus clouds drifting from south to north. Frank Thorne was seated at a table on his poolside deck, reading a magazine and working on a gin and tonic when Doyle and Billy walked up. "So what'd their art expert have to say?" he asked.

Doyle rolled his eyes as the two sat. "What a flamin' blowhard. Little sucker prattled on for over an hour. Must've been charging by the word. I had to leave in the middle and come back for the thrilling finale. I'm still trying to wake up."

Frank looked at Billy. "You stayed?"

"Through the whole thing."

"So, what'd he say?"

"Took him forever, but he ended up saying the painting is legit, of course."

Frank stared at him for a second, then turned to Doyle.

"That's pretty much it," Doyle agreed. "He said it's the real thing."

Frank turned to Billy. "Good. Good job."

"Thanks, Pop."

Frank reached for his drink but suddenly froze. "I'm assumin' the buyer's bringin' cash, right?"

"Yeah, it's a cash deal," Billy said. "But I got something I want to run past you."

Frank glanced up. "Yeah? What's that?"

"I know it's a little last minute, but we got another opportunity, sort of a parlay."

Frank glanced at Doyle, who shrugged.

"I ran across a guy," Billy said. "Dude's in the energy business over in Bellevue."

"Oil and gas energy? That kind of thing?"

"Better. This is *clean* energy."

* * * *

"So, *that's* what's behind the art deal," Billy said as he finished explaining the encounter at the racetrack, the test he'd attended at Emerald Fusion Technology, and the opportunity to buy into the company. "The way it would go is we sell the painting to this art collector Velazquez for two million cash. Then we take the cash and invest it in Emerald Fusion Technology. A week later, we get paid back, with a big, fat return."

Frank slowly set down his drink. He scowled, then said, "What I'm really hearing is that there ain't no deal to buy the painting unless we agree to put the money into this energy company. That sounds like a scam."

Billy held up his hands. "No, that's not right, Pop. We sell the painting for cash. We can do what we want with the money. The investment is a separate deal. I'm just sayin' it's another opportunity, an even bigger opportunity, to make a huge pile of money here." Billy let that sink in and then continued. "But if you're not interested, this Velazquez guy wants the painting, one way or another."

Doyle nodded. "He *was* crazy about it, boss."

"Tell me what I'm missin' here," Frank said. "If we can turn half a million into two million by selling the painting, what the hell's wrong with that? That's pretty close to a sure thing. And in ninety days? I call that a helluva good deal. What's wrong with leaving it at that?"

Billy said, "Nothing. Nothing wrong with it at all. And it *is* a good deal, if I say so myself. It was *me* who arranged it, after all." He leaned forward slightly. "But there's a couple things I think you might be missin'."

"Do tell."

"First is ten-to-one."

"Ten-to-one?" Frank glanced at his heavy gold Rolex and noted that it was four fifteen, then he said, "What? Something happen at ten-to-one that I should know about?"

"Ten-to-one *return*, Pop," Billy interrupted. "On the entire two mil." Billy explained the opportunity to fund the stock options and then collect when the company sold to Matsumoro.

"Matsumoro," Doyle mused. "I think I heard of them."

"Damn right. They're legit," Billy agreed. "Nigel looked 'em up. They're, like, this huge industrial conglomerate thing."

"And they're coming on Saturday to close the deal for a hundred mil?" Frank asked. "And this . . . machine? It works?"

Billy nodded. "Sure the hell does. Nigel and I saw it."

Frank stared at him, then a moment later, he said, "What's the other thing?"

"What?"

"The other thing. You said there were a couple of things I'm missin'."

Billy smiled. "Oh! The second one's probably more important. Consider this, Pop." He smiled. "None of these other neighbor geeks around here know about this opportunity. None of 'em got the chance to identify an up-and-comin' company and take advantage of the situation. None of 'em are gonna cash in on it on the ground floor, like it's the next Apple Computer or the next Google or somethin'. We can beat 'em to the punch. Who's the smart one now, right? And *that's* the kind of thing that's bound to hit the business news. Hell, if you want, you'll be able to change the company's name from Thorne Financial to Thorne Venture Capital overnight! Talk about legit!"

Frank stared at him, the issue hanging in the air. Finally, he said, "Besides you, who've we got who's seen this . . . this *machine* work?"

"Just me and Nigel." Billy studied his father's reaction. "And I'm guessing we don't count."

"Not unless one of you got a PhD you never told me about."

"It's just been the two of us so far."

"That ain't good enough to risk two million bucks. If we do this thing, we need our own expert, somebody that *we're* paying. We need him to see another test, to look out for us."

"Oh," Billy said, taking a quick breath. "The Japanese will be there on Saturday. We'd have to get someone in before then."

Frank said, "So we need someone on short notice. Somebody other than you and Nigel."

It was quiet for a few seconds.

"Hey!" Billy said, sitting upright. He reached for his wallet and pulled a business card out and flipped it onto the table. "I might have someone for you."

Frank picked it up and read the name. "Sean Flannery, PhD."

"Keep readin'," Billy said.

"Chairman of the Experimental Nuclear Physics section at the Physics Department, University of Washington." Frank studied the card, then he nodded. He looked up at Billy. "Call him up."

* * * *

The new command room hidden at the back of the Emerald Fusion Technology lab was dominated by three large computer monitors. The constant drone of electronics-cooling fans masked the sounds coming from outside the lab. Overhead, a row of smaller monitors cycled through video cameras placed inside and outside the lab.

Kenny Hale and Murphy Thompson were seated at a long table in front of the monitors, talking to Henry and Lulu about the details of the software programming in the lab and the observation room when, suddenly, a black phone rang—two shorts and a long.

"Hey!" Kenny said. "Two shorts and a long, look here on the screen. It's Billy Thorne." He turned to Henry. "You called it."

"He calling for U-Dub?" Henry asked.

"Yeah. I programmed it so that's all that rings through."

Henry rubbed his hands together. "Perfect. You guys ready?"

Kenny nodded. Murphy took a deep breath, then nodded.

"Do it," Henry said.

Kenny selected an app on the computer screen in front of him, and a script popped up on his monitor. Then he clicked on another button on the screen and a phone between the monitors rang. He answered, "University of Washington Physics Department." A pause, then, "Who's that? Professor Flannery? Yeah, he's around here somewhere. Hold on for a second. I'll see if I can track him down."

He placed the call on hold, then he punched another button, and ambient industrial sounds like those heard in a factory, or perhaps in a nuclear physics lab, played from his computer speakers. When twenty seconds had passed, he pointed to Murphy. "You're on." He turned the volume up.

"Physics Lab One!" she barked into the phone over the background noise. "Dr. Flannery? I think he's .... yeah, I can see him. He's running a mass spectrometer test right now. Can I take a note and have him call you?"

A second later, she added, "Okay. Billy Thorne. Yeah, I got it. Okay, I will." She hung up and turned to Kenny, who turned off the ambient sounds. Murphy smiled and handed the note to Henry. "Piece of cake. Mr. Thorne would like the good doctor to give him a call."

Henry beamed. "Nice job, guys. Now, wasn't that fun? We'll make first-class grifters out of the both of you."

Kenny and Murphy high-fived each other.

CHAPTER 24

The Convincer

"Dr. Sean!" Johnny said with glee.

Real-life Professor Conner Farrell was dressed for the part—a tweed jacket, tan slacks, dark Oxfords, and a thin leather attaché case. "Well, lookee here," he said in his thick Irish brogue as he shook Johnny's hand. He smiled broadly like a proud parent. "So, you've gone and proved me wrong and made something of yourself after all, have ya? Who'da guessed?"

Johnny laughed. "Always said I would."

"Aye, that you did," the professor said. "It's just, no one ever believed ya." He turned to Billy. "You must be Mr. Thorne, then." He shook Billy's hand. "Sean Flannery. Thanks for the call. I've been wantin' to see this machine for myself."

"So," Billy said, nodding toward Johnny, "he was your student?"

"Aye, he was. Had the misfortune of having him take up

space in my lab for six *long* years before I could finally get him out of there. A real challenge, this one. But look at him now." He nodded toward the lab. "Look what they've done."

"That's about enough," Johnny said. He turned to Billy. "He's putting you on. I'm the best student he ever had, and he knows it."

The professor shrugged. "Could be. But you never heard it from me. We don't need him to get all swell-headed."

"Very true," Johnny said. He greeted Nigel, then he turned to Doyle. "I see Billy's brought reinforcements this morning."

"Doyle Reese," Doyle said. "I work for Billy's father, and I'm here to watch."

"Good," Johnny said excitedly. He put his hand on the professor's shoulder. "I didn't think the boss was going to authorize another test run so close to the big demo on Saturday, but when he found out this guy was going to be here, he changed his mind. I think he's anxious to show off LEO."

"Damn right, I am," Henry said as he entered the lobby with Buttons. He smiled broadly. "Dr. Flannery, good to see you again." The two shook hands, and Henry said, "Allow me to introduce Larry McElroy from James Street Global Energy. So, what's it been? Three, four years since the particle accelerator conference in New York?"

"Aye, about that."

Henry turned to Billy. "Good morning, Mr. Thorne. I see you've brought Doctor Flannery here to check us out. Fair enough. I think we're about ready. What say we get this show on the road."

****

An hour later, the test was concluded, and everyone had moved back to the lobby, happy with the results. During the test, the team had run the power up and delivered a new record COP ratio of 6.0.

"Simply amazin'," the professor said, shaking his head. "I'da never believed COP at six-plus without seein' it with my own eyes. It's remarkable."

"What'd I tell you?" Henry smiled broadly. "The more input power we put to it, the exponentially higher the output."

"I should say. I—"

"Say," Billy interrupted. He looked at the professor. "Professor, we got another appointment we have to get to. You mind steppin' outside with us for a second?"

The men walked outside.

When the door swung closed, Billy said, "So, you think this thing's legit?"

The professor nodded enthusiastically. "I'd have never believed it, but there it is, right in front of us. I saw it with my own two eyes."

"No shenanigans?"

"None that I could see. I checked everywhere they'da needed to have monkeyed with things to show the results they're showing, but everything was clean. I can't see where they've altered anything at all. No hidden power sources, no bogus calorimeter methodology, nothing like that. They're definitely turning hydrogen into helium and releasing a ton of heat in the process.

It's damn amazing, isn't it? I don't know how they do it without releasing a huge load of gamma rays, but the radiation release is practically nil. I took notes. I can send you a report."

"So, you think it's got value, then?" Doyle asked. "I mean, the company says they're bringing the Japanese in to buy this whole setup for a hundred million dollars. That's a big number. That make sense to you?"

The professor laughed. "I'm a scientist, not a businessman. I make no claim about understanding economics. But I can say that I've been in this business for thirty years now, and every so often, something comes along that changes the way we think about things, something that has a real impact, ya know? Disruptive, even. I don't know the numbers, but all I can say is . . . yeah, it sure seems like it could be a helluva investment. Worth billions, even.

"In fact, along these lines, if ya don't mind, I'd like to talk to them about seeing if they'll carve me out a little ownership piece. I don't have huge money—nothin' like you guys—but I've got a retirement account that I can tap. I think it'd be a good idea to throw some money behind this before it gets all kinds of crazy, which I'm thinkin' this thing is about to do. Once word gets out, it's going to be big."

"Long as they don't cut us back," Billy said. He pulled out his wallet and peeled off ten hundred-dollar bills. "Here you go, Doc. Your consulting fee. Thanks."

* * * *

"So? Another good test," Johnny said to Billy and Nigel. They stood in the Emerald Fusion lobby, talking with Danny and Toni as they watched the professor drive away. "What do you guys think?"

"Impressive," Billy said.

"Damn right, it is." Johnny gestured toward the professor's car. "What'd *he* say?"

"He said he's gonna talk to you guys about gettin' in."

Johnny laughed. "I think that's what he was doing in there just before he left. Everyone wants in now—now that we're so close."

"Well," Billy said. "We're in for sure. Let's go talk to your boss and get things finalized."

"Great! I'm glad to hear it. Let's go talk to—"

He was interrupted as four men walked in. All were dressed similarly, in dark suits. Each man had a short haircut, and all had serious looks on their faces.

"Good morning," the man in front said. "Who's in charge?"

Johnny looked the men over. "That'd be me."

"Are you . . ." The man looked down to refer to a small black notebook he carried. "Are you Myles Cohen?"

Johnny shook his head. "No, he's in the back. Who are you guys, anyway?"

The man reached into his pocket and pulled out a wallet, flipping it open with a practiced nonchalance to reveal an ID card and a badge. "My name is Special Agent Leavitt and this is Special Agent Spelling. We're with the FBI Seattle Field Office. These other gentlemen here are both inspectors with the Department of Energy. We'd like to speak to Myles Cohen."

* * * *

"Dammit," Johnny whispered as he watched Henry lead the men back to his office. "I knew we pushed the power too hard."

"What do you mean?" Danny asked. He and Billy stood next to Johnny in the lobby.

"Some engineer at the power company must have noticed the spike when we ran the test a couple of days ago. Now the feds are jumping in."

"Shhh!" Lulu whispered. "Listen . . ."

"Myles Cohen, we're here to inform you that we believe you may be in violation of the Atomic Energy Act of 1954." Special Agent Leavitt's voice was clear as he started speaking in Henry's office. "With this notice that I'm giving you now, you are hereby warned that you must immediately cease and desist any and all illegal activities connected with unlicensed nuclear power generation here until your complete operation has been reviewed and properly licensed by the DOE."

"Nuclear power generation?" Henry demanded. "What nuclear power generation? You got it all wrong, pal. We've got no nuclear power generation going on here."

"You work with fusion, correct?" Special Agent Leavitt asked.

"Yeah, what of it?"

"So that means you combine nuclei from a light element, and you end up with nuclei in a heavier element. The laws of physics say when that happens, energy is released—energy that can take the form of radiation."

"Think Three Mile Island," Special Agent Spelling said.

"My ass!" Henry protested. "Laws of physics? Whose laws of physics? Yours? Mine? The government's? Just because they say so? Gentlemen, you know the so-called laws of physics really refer to 'what we've observed so far.' When we observe something new, the laws are adjusted to accommodate. Physics isn't bound by a government definition."

"Well, that may be true," Leavitt said, "but for the time being, *you* are. The 1954 act deals with the release of radiation, and that's where we come in."

Henry stared at the man. "This is crap! We monitor carefully. You want to try and shut us down, we're going to fight you on it."

"That's your right. But meanwhile, you are potentially exposing this entire area to a huge radiation hazard if something goes wrong. That's against the law."

"Think Fukushima," one of the DOE inspectors added.

"This is bullshit," Henry said. "We've run our experiment dozens of times. There's never been any release of radiation."

"Look," one of the DOE men said. "We're done talking here. You get one warning, and this is it. I'm leaving you a copy of the official cease-and-desist order here. You wanna appeal, make the proper application to the DOE office in Seattle. But I'm telling you, if you don't do that and if we have to come back, we'll be shutting this company down. Permanently."

"And," Special Agent Leavitt added, "if that happens, the Department of Justice will be pursuing criminal charges against you and any other owners of this company who violate this order. So just keep that in mind. Have a nice day."

The four men left the stunned group of listeners, walked out the door, hopped in their sedan, and drove away.

* * * *

Buttons walked up to Henry while he was still in the lobby, watching the "DOE" vehicle leave the parking area. "Myles, much as I hate to say it, I'm afraid this changes things for us. James Street is going to have to take a pass until you get this sorted out with the DOE."

Henry spun around. "A pass? The demo with Matsumoro is tomorrow! You mean you're out? Because of those guys?"

"Those *guys*, as you put it, are the FBI *and* the DOE, and they're ordering you to stop. That's good enough for me."

"Ah, come on, Larry," Henry protested. "They're full of crap. You know that! We don't produce any radiation here. If we have to, we'll fight 'em, and we'll win. What we're doing is too important for those bureaucrats to shut down. You know that."

"What I know is that James Street is a highly regulated business. I've got the SEC watching us with a microscope nearly 24/7. Whatever we do, whatever we get involved in, it's gonna get looked at, and that means it's got to be squeaky clean, beyond reproach. Otherwise, *we* run the risk of getting shut down ourselves. And, as much as I like your project, there's no single deal that's worth getting shut down over. Get it handled, then we talk about coming in. Meanwhile, I've got no choice in this matter."

Buttons and his assistant collected their belongings and exited.

CHAPTER 25

The Squeeze

Henry shook his head as he watched the James Street entourage load up and drive away. "Great, that's just great. One day away from wrapping up the biggest deal of my life, and now this. With all we've been through? What's it gonna be next? Pestilence? The plague?"

"Can they do that?" Johnny asked. "The feds? Can they just swing in here and threaten us like that? Force us to close our business?"

Henry took a slow deep breath, then he grimaced. "They just did. We're dead in the water."

"Shut down?" Billy said. "Done?" He pointed to the laboratory observation window. "All this is just over? Just like that?"

"Those guys were the feds, pal. Yeah, I'd say it's over," Henry said, taking off his lab coat.

"Wait a second, Myles," Danny said. "This isn't right.

It sounds like garbage to me. You guys aren't doing anything wrong. They can't just waltz in here and shut you down based on something that they *think might* happen." He reached for his cell phone. "My dad's a lawyer. I'm gonna ask him to come in on this and have a look. You can't just give up without fighting these bastards."

"Danny's right," Johnny added. "We've got to fight them."

Henry held up his hand. "Hold up, there. I appreciate all of your concern, I really do. But before you go calling in the cavalry, you guys are all missing the bigger point. Far as it goes, I don't mind fighting the feds. Hell, I've done a fair amount of that in my life. If it was just a question of duking it out with them over their legal crap, I'm sure we'd kick their butts. Eventually. But doing it takes time, and *that's* the real problem."

"The pencil-pushing skinny-tie bastards had to show up today at the exact same moment the James Street guys were here. Ten minutes later and they'd have missed them. But they didn't, and now we're stuck. James Street is out for now, doesn't matter if we fight it or not. Matsumoro's coming in to wrap up the purchase tomorrow morning. They're coming a long way, and they're expecting to see a fully functional LEO 2.0. We're all set to work an all-nighter to get ready. I've got a ton of parts arriving this afternoon—palladium, deuterium. Hell, even two industrial generators I was going to put in the parking lot to supply the power and keep us totally off the grid. But all that stuff's expensive. I've been counting on four million bucks this afternoon from James Street to pay for it. And to be honest, I've been getting used to the idea of another two million from Mr.

Thorne's oil painting here on top of that. Now I'm gonna have to send it all back. If we can't pay for it, we can't build it. Can't build it, can't show it. Can't show it, can't sell it. Which means, basically, we're screwed!" He turned and kicked the wall. "Damn!"

The room was silent as everyone absorbed his words. Then Lulu said, "Myles, are we really that critical on cash?"

"You mean, can we cover the loss of six million bucks?" He shook his head. "I wish." Henry looked around helplessly. "I'm gonna have to call them up and tell 'em not to come, if it's not already too late." He turned and walked down the hall to his office, shutting the door behind him.

* * * *

Ten minutes later, Danny and Toni were outside in the parking lot, talking with Johnny and Billy.

"Look," Toni said. "I know it's not much, but Danny and I have 401(k)s. We could probably put in a hundred thousand together. We could have it on Monday."

Danny turned to look at her. "We can do that?"

"Yeah," she said. "It's not six million bucks, but maybe it would pay for the generators."

Billy shrugged. "I already said I'd put in the two million from selling the painting. That hasn't changed."

Johnny tilted his head. "You mean you'd still be willing to stay in? Even now? Even with the feds?"

"Feds?" Billy said with a smirk. "Hell yeah. Feds don't scare me."

"I'm sure Myles assumed that with James Street bailing, you'd be out, too."

"He assumed wrong. We could stay in. But . . . things are riskier now with the feds all over things. We'd have to get thirty percent instead of twenty."

Johnny stared at him. "Talk about kicking someone when they're down. That could mean another ten million bucks for you on the payday. At best, that's going to piss Myles off. We had a deal."

Billy shrugged. "Well, he doesn't have to do it, then. He can find some other investors. Oh wait, snap! His other investors just drove away." Billy laughed. "Face it. The risk has gone up—way the hell up. The feds are threatening to bust all the owners. Why would you expect any sane investor to jump right into the middle of that frying pan without some additional compensation? That deserves something, right? Besides, it's a helluva lot better than nothing."

Johnny continued to stare at him.

"So," Billy said, "what do you say? Can you guys make it happen with two million?"

"Two-point-one," Toni said.

"I don't know," Johnny said. "Let's go find out."

* * * *

"Two-point-one million dollars," Henry said, tapping a pencil on the desk while he stared at the ceiling.

The group was reassembled in his office.

"Two-point-one," he said again. "If I don't count the two from the painting, which was kind of unexpected anyway, I was originally expecting four from the James Street fund. With the painting, we'd be halfway home."

He looked at Billy and said, "So the feds don't scare you off? I thought you'd be out of here by now."

Billy shook his head. "My family's dealt with feds before—lots of times, actually."

Henry resumed staring at the ceiling and tapping his pencil.

"Two-point-one. It might be possible. Maybe." He stopped and gave a big smile. "With a couple million, I can probably get the suppliers to float the balance until next week after Matsumoro closes." He smiled. "Hell, it's worth a shot, right?"

Johnny nodded enthusiastically. "Great!"

"Hold on a second, though," Billy said. "The way I see it, the risk has gone up. Way the hell up. Which is why our price has gone up. We put up two million in cash, we want thirty percent of the stock."

Henry froze. His smile vanished. "Say again?"

"We go from twenty to thirty percent."

Henry's face hardened. A menacing smile slowly appeared. "Mr. Thorne, I've got a stock-option deal with Jimmy—two million for twenty percent. *Twenty*. Period. If you can't live with that, I guess this means that our discussion here has come to an end. Hit the road, pal."

Billy was shocked. "What?"

"You heard me." Henry slowly got to his feet and nodded toward the door. "Out. You don't come in my office and try to blackmail me when you think I'm up against the wall. Door's over there. I got work to do."

"Whoa!" Billy said. "Hold up there." He forced a smile. "We're just negotiating here."

"Negotiating?" Henry said. "You got a funny way of negotiating. You don't start by insulting someone's intelligence."

"I didn't insult your intelligence," Billy protested. "If this is your way of saying you don't like my offer, then shoot me a counteroffer. But don't just sit there and get pissed."

"Counteroffer?" Henry said. "I don't need a counter. Far as I'm concerned, we already have a deal."

"We *did* have a deal," Billy insisted. "Till the feds showed up. Now we gotta have a new deal. Have you considered that thirty percent to us still leaves you with seventy percent of the company if you guys can make it work? That's a lot better than you were gonna end up with the hedge fund, right?"

Henry glowered, but after a few seconds, he said, "True. Okay. Twenty-five. Twenty-five percent of the company for two million and not a penny more."

Billy smiled. "Okay. Twenty-five it is."

* * * *

"Don't look now, but we're being watched," Danny said, opening the car door for Toni as they left the lab.

"Where?"

"Parking lot to the west, about seventy-five yards away. Dark blue sedan. One guy inside."

Toni slid into her seat, and Danny walked around the car and hopped in.

"You got any idea who it might be?" she asked.

"I don't know. Maybe it's Farley Palmer."

Toni considered this for a moment, then she said, "If it's Palmer, then he's getting too close. I mean, the big show is tomorrow. I wonder if he's somehow made the connection?" She turned to him as they pulled away. "Danny, we've got to tell Henry."

He made the turn out of the drive and said, "You're right. I'll call him."

CHAPTER 26

Final Plans

"Good news and bad news," Billy said. It was late Friday afternoon, and he and Doyle were in Frank's office, reporting on the results of the test. "Good news for us. Bad news for Myles Cohen."

"What happened?"

"First, the good news," Billy said. "The test went fine."

"It did," Doyle agreed. "It's pretty damn amazing, boss. Those scientists over there have put together some kind of operation. They have this old building at the end of 22nd. Doesn't look like much from the outside, but inside, they've got this state-of-the-art lab. They've invented this LEONARDO thing. It's friggin' mind-blowing."

"What'd your physics professor say?"

Billy smiled. "He's gonna send us a report. He watched the whole demonstration. Poked, prodded, asked questions. Get this—when it was all done, he said he was gonna run right down and cash out his retirement account so he could invest. He wants in. He called it a game changer."

Doyle added, "He said the Japanese wouldn't come in unless they think they'll make billions on it."

"Billions?"

"Yeah, with a 'b'."

"Same thing those two local PIs said," said Billy. "They wanna jump in with their 401(k)s, too. Small potatoes, but not to them. Bottom line—everyone who sees this thing wants in."

Frank pursed his lips for a few moments. Then he said, "So what's the bad news?"

"The bad news is that after the test was over, the feds showed up—FBI and DOE both," Billy said. "They read Cohen the riot act and started threatening people. Said he had to 'cease and desist.'"

"Why?"

"Bunch of legal bullshit, regulation this, regulation that," Billy said. He explained what had happened.

After he'd heard it all, Frank said, "This so-called legal bullshit—why shouldn't we be worried about it? The feds put people in prison over so-called legal bullshit, ya know. They're good at it. Sounds like those other investors were concerned. Why shouldn't we be concerned, too?"

"Because Cohen *knew* the feds were likely to be lurking about. He was already planning to run the Japanese demo using generators that he's bringing in this afternoon. He knew he needed to be off-grid. The feds would never see it, the Japanese would, the deal closes."

"But now you're telling me the damage is done. He lost his investors? How's he gonna pay for the demo?"

"He just presumed we were gonna bail, too. When he found out we weren't scared off, then he got creative. He figures that by using the money from the sale of the painting, and then putting off paying his suppliers for a few days, they're good. In other words, he figured out a way to get around it."

Frank considered this. He stared at his desk for a minute, then he looked up. "You know, this makes us the only chicken in the oven. If we do the deal, there's a lot more risk. You shoulda got something outta this."

"I did," Billy said, a smug look on his face. "I told him just that, that our risk had gone up. I told him we needed compensation—thirty percent. He about threw me out, so we ended up settling for twenty-five percent. Which means I made us another five million bucks on the deal. Now I think we should be up to a twenty-five-million return on our original five-hundred-thousand investment."

He turned to Doyle. "Doyle, help me out here. What kind of return rate is that? Fifty-to-one? Holy crap!" he said, mugging. "Can that be right?"

"Stop gloating," Frank said. He leaned back in his chair and pursed his lips. A moment later, he sat up suddenly. "Anyone heard from Farley Palmer recently? I ain't talked to him for a couple of days."

"Not me," Billy said. "But he don't have much to say to me, anyways."

Doyle shook his head. "Me neither, boss."

Frank turned to Doyle. "Track that son of a bitch down. Tell 'em I need to talk to him. Right now."

"Tonight still?" Doyle asked.

"Yeah, tonight," Frank said. "Why not? Tomorrow's the deal—it'll be too late. When'd you think I meant?"

"Sorry. It's just I knew you got the party set for tonight."

Frank looked at the office door, then shot him a glare. "Shhh! Keep your voice down, will ya, Doyle? I ain't asked her yet, and she ain't said yes yet."

"C'mon, boss, 'course she'll say yes."

Frank glanced at Billy and saw the question in his eyes.

"Tonight's the night," he said, smiling. "Got the ring back this morning and I'm poppin' the question to Lorraine later. Then, after she says yes, we're gonna have us a little celebration party—all of us."

Billy's face was expressionless for a moment, then he forced a smile. "That's great, Pop. Great." He paused, then said, "So, what about the deal?"

Frank nodded. "All right. If you still believe in it, let's do it."

* * * *

Danny and Toni were seated at the table in Henry's hotel suite at six thirty in the evening.

"We're worried that Farley Palmer might be putting things together," Danny said.

"And if he does," Toni said, "we're worried that he'll notify the Thornes, and then we'll have a real problem."

"Really?" Henry asked as he poured a bottle of water into a glass full of ice. "What's got you so concerned?"

"We think someone was watching us when we did the test today," Toni said.

"Yeah?"

"Yeah – someone was parked in the next lot. We're afraid it might be Palmer," Danny said.

Henry considered this for a moment, then he said, "You couldn't make him out?"

Danny shook his head. "Not without giving ourselves away. We didn't want to stare too long or confront him. So far, he doesn't know we've noticed him."

Henry nodded as he thought for a moment. "What is it that makes you think it might be Palmer and that he might be watching you? Whoever it is could be watching Billy Thorne. Hell, it could be someone from a nearby office eating their lunch. I doubt Farley Palmer is checking out the lab. Besides, even if he is, I'm not worried about it. I don't think there's any way he's discovered a connection between Kate and Ray and Emerald Fusion. I think we should relax. I'm certain the Thornes haven't made the connection."

"Glad *you're* not worried," Toni said. "How can you be so sure?"

Henry smiled. "Simple. No one's shooting at us."

THE
RAIN CITY HUSTLE

CHAPTER 27

Morning

A morning breeze stirred the water across Lake Union into gentle chop before making its way up the slope to Danny and Toni's apartment, where Toni sat outside at a patio table, drinking a cup of coffee and staring absently at the lake. A few moments later, Danny bounded up the steps from the street. He was breathing hard, and his shirt was soaked with sweat. He punched a button on his watch, checked his time, and reached for the towel and the water bottle that Toni handed him.

"Thanks." He quickly downed half the bottle.

Toni looked up. "All better?"

"What's that?" He buried his face in the towel.

"I said, 'all better?' You tossed and turned all night long, and I'm wondering if a hard training run helped clear your head."

He wrapped the towel around his shoulders and smiled. "Yeah, I'm good."

"Nervous?"

"Yeah, I suppose. A little anyway. Aren't you?"

Toni shook her head. "No, not really. Henry and Johnny seem to know what they're doing. Long as Farley Palmer doesn't show up."

"Henry's probably right—no reason for him to."

"I know. But still, it'll be nice to get this all wrapped up. Just think—in another couple of hours, Kate will have her painting back and we'll be 'mission accomplished'. And, if all goes well, the Thornes will be none the wiser."

"It's called karma. That's what they get for trying to steal the painting from Kate. It'll be a good lesson for them."

"You really think they'll learn a lesson from this?"

Danny took a quick breath, then shook his head. "Nah, they don't seem like teachable types. But they brought all this on themselves."

"True."

He took a step closer to her and smiled. "So . . . we finish up, get this little diversion behind us, then we can get down to the important business next week."

She smiled. "Rehearsal . . . wedding . . . honeymoon in Hawaii."

Danny leaned down to kiss her.

After a moment, she pushed him away. "You'd better hit the shower. You smell like a marathon runner."

* * * *

"You all packed up, Dad?" Lulu said to Henry as she looked over his bags upon entering his suite. "Johnny's all set to call the bell desk."

"Just about." Henry was in the living room, standing before a mirror, working on his tie. "I'm having a little trouble with this damn thing . . . again." He shook his hand. "I think my arthritis is acting up."

"Here," Lulu said, "let me help you." She walked over and started working on his tie. "Good thing you got me around."

Henry nodded. "No disagreement there."

Lulu noticed the photo of Henry and her mother, along with Aunt Mary and Uncle Harold, that Henry had placed on the desk in the suite's living room. She paused for a moment, then said, "Don't forget mom's picture."

"Not a chance."

She finished his tie and stepped back. "Perfect."

Henry looked in the mirror, then he nodded.

"Are we all set then?" Lulu asked.

Henry took a deep breath, then he nodded. "We are. We move fast—"

Lulu smiled. "And stay one step ahead."

* * * *

"Billy!" Chloe reached over and nudged Billy. "Billy, wake up! I thought today was supposed to be your big day. What about your meeting this morning?"

Billy stirred. "Huh? Leave me alone." Then, groaning, he added, "My stomach feels like a buffalo stampede ran me over."

"I know. You were up all night. I heard the others leave for the club a couple of hours ago. I didn't want to wake you. But don't you have your meeting this morning?" she said, lifting her head and looking at the clock. "Was it canceled?"

Billy worked his eyes open and squinted at the clock on the nightstand beside his bed. Suddenly, his eyes opened wide, and he sat up straight. "Oh crap!" he said, pulling the covers off Chloe. He stood up but immediately leaned forward and clutched his stomach.

"Hey!" She grabbed the blankets and covered herself. Then she looked over at him. "You okay?"

He shook his head. "No. Last night . . . oh man."

"I told you. It was all those oysters you and Ernie were slamming. I think they must have been bad."

"Perfect." He reached for his robe and wobbled slightly as someone knocked on the door.

"Billy!" Nigel called from outside. "Wakey-wakey!"

Billy walked slowly to the door and opened it. Nigel started to speak but stopped when he saw Billy's face. He smiled broadly and looked at him with amusement.

"So, you're *not* ready. You forget we're supposed to deliver the painting"—he looked at his watch—"thirty minutes from now?"

Billy groaned. "No. I got a messed-up stomach from last night."

"You and Ernie both. I just left him at the club with your old man. He's got a screamin' dose of the trots."

"I did, too. All night. Better now, but still."

"So that's why you missed breakfast at the club."

"Damn right. Do I look like I should be having breakfast at the country club?" He glanced at a nearby clock. "Do me a favor. While I get ready, go grab the painting from the study. Then pull the car around to the side here."

* * * *

The *Fade to Crimson* set was busy, crew members hustling about, setting up gear, moving back and forth between the equipment trailer and the set. People were smiling and chatting among themselves about the morning's upcoming closing shot.

Near the set, Ray LeGrande was huddled over a video monitor, sharing a joke with a cheerful brunette, his hand resting on her thigh. Kate was nearly upon him before he noticed. She walked up, accompanied by two men—one older, silver-haired, and dressed in a charcoal business suit, the other younger, prematurely balding, wearing jeans and a denim vest over a white shirt.

Ray's smile melted away when he saw Kate approach. He quickly stood up. "Kate," he said. Then he noticed the two men. "What are you doing here?" he said to the young man.

Kate smiled. "Good. You remember Rollie Berghoff, then?" Before he could answer, she continued. "You're about to shoot the final shot, correct?"

He nodded. "Yeah . . ."

"Good." She handed him an envelope. "Ray, after this final

shot, you're out—no longer employed by or otherwise any part of this company."

"What?" Ray stared at her for a moment, his mouth agape. "You can't do that! We're not done! We have post to get through!"

"The company does. *You* don't." She stared at him. "We're done, Ray. No more: you and the company, you and me. Done."

Ray's face reddened. "C'mon, Kate! Is this because of last night? I told you yesterday I'd be working late."

She shook her head. "Save it. It's too late. Here's the deal. *If* you behave—*if* you finish up and cooperate through post—I'll see that you get the director credits and a fifty percent share of whatever profits I can wring out of this, minus Danny Logan's fee for recovering the painting—that's all on you. But one way or the other, today's the end. Rollie's going to take the film through post-production." She turned to the brunette. "You're out, too. Immediately. Find someone else's husband to edit."

Ray's mouth dropped. "You can't just walk in here and do this!"

"Yes, I can." She turned to the man in the suit. "Ted?"

The silver-haired man nodded. "I'm afraid she can, Mr. LeGrande. You're both officers in the production company, but one hundred percent of the stock belongs to Kate and her father. Which means she can convene a special meeting of the board for purposes of removing you, which she did this morning. Such actions are solely at her discretion. She has total control."

Kate nodded. "So . . . finish up. And you," she said, turning to the brunette, "get off my set."

* * * *

In a small, sparsely furnished apartment in the Capitol Hill area of Seattle, Farley Palmer grabbed his black notebook and stuffed it in a pocket. He glanced at his watch. Then he picked up his car keys, his wallet, and his leather sap from the counter. At the front door, he turned for a final check and looked around. He took a deep breath, then he shut the door behind him.

CHAPTER 28

Lab Time

At ten twenty-five, Emerald Fusion was alive with activity. White-coated "scientists" and "technicians" were swarming over the new device in the lab when Billy Thorne walked into the lobby, accompanied by Nigel, who carried a large art case.

"Morning, Mr. Thorne," Henry said. He rubbed his hands together. "Big day today."

"Yeah." Billy looked around. "Busy around here. Any word from Matsumoro?"

"They called. They landed at Boeing fifteen minutes ago. They're on the way."

"Got something we can set this on?" Billy asked, nodding toward the art case. "Velazquez is gonna want to have another look."

Henry had Lulu bring out an easel. Nigel removed the

painting from the case and set it up in a corner of the lobby.

"So," Billy said, "here it is. Now all we need is our buyer."

"I'm here!" Sal said as he walked into the lobby, assistant in tow. He made a beeline directly to the painting. "Oh my! When I'm away, I forget just how magnificent it is." He admired the painting for several moments, hands clasped, saying nothing.

Danny suppressed a smile as he leaned toward Toni. "He looks like a man who's been chasing a dream with a butterfly net his whole life and finally caught it," he whispered.

Sal turned to Billy. "Are you ready? May we start?"

Billy nodded. "Hell yeah. Let's get this wrapped up before the Japanese get here."

"The Japanese?" Sal said.

"It's a separate deal," Toni said. "Not related."

"Oh." He turned to his assistant and said, "Well, shall we?"

The two quickly went through a checklist and "reverified" the painting as authentic. Five minutes later, they were through.

Sal smiled. He reached into his breast pocket and pulled out an envelope. "Perfect. Just as agreed, I have a certified check in the amount of two million dollars. If you have the paperwork, we can turn this over to you now."

Henry nodded. "Let's do—"

"Hold up there a minute."

Danny quickly turned around. His mouth dropped when Frank Thorne and Doyle Reese walked through the doors into the lobby.

* * * *

Henry stared at Frank for a moment, then said, "Who the hell are you?"

"My name is Frank Thorne."

"*Frank* Thorne?" Henry considered this, then looked at Billy, who quickly lowered his eyes. "Frank Thorne? Who's this, Thorne? Your old man? What'd you do? Bring him along so he could sign off on the deal? Hell, I could've just sent you home with a permission slip, ya know." He glanced at Frank. "Saved you the trip."

Billy, looking completely befuddled, said, "Pop, what's going on?"

"I got this, Bill," Frank said. He turned back to Henry. "I understand you've been speaking to my son about a certain investment in your company."

Henry narrowed his eyes. "Yeah, I have. And to be frank, Frank, we expected to be swapping a cashier's check for the painting here right about now. The buyer—Mr. Velazquez—he's ready to close. I thought we had a deal."

"Well," Frank said, "about that. I'm here with a *new* deal."

"Geez!" Henry said. "What is it with this Thorne family and their 'new deals'?"

Danny glanced at Toni, eyebrows raised. She gave him a barely perceptible shrug.

"I understand you've lost your investors," Frank said. "Your James Street hedge fund boys got themselves a little squeamish over problems of, shall we say, a federal nature."

"Yeah?" Henry said. "What's it to ya? We got that all worked out." He glanced at Billy. "Least I *thought* we had it all worked out."

"Relax, Mr. Cohen," Frank said. "I'm not here to trip you up. In fact, I'm here to solve your problem. We've studied your operation, and we want in—my company wants in. Thorne Venture Capital is in the finance business, ya see? And—here's the good part—we don't want in for just the two million for the painting. We'll do that, plus we'll take the entire four million piece that the hedge fund was gonna cover—a total of six million. You won't have to worry about how to pay your suppliers while you wait for the Japanese money to come through."

"Six million?" Henry looked at him for a moment, then he shrugged. "Sorry, pal. I don't know you, and besides, I don't need your four million. After the fund backed out yesterday, I worked with the suppliers. I got 'em to agree to accept half now, half next week when the Japanese come through. So we're good. We don't need your four mil."

"Fair enough," Frank said. "Then we'll just pack up the painting and leave." He nodded to Doyle. "Looks like we'll be going to that auction in New York next week after all."

Danny rocked backwards, his eyes open wide.

"Hey!" Sal protested. "I thought we had a deal!"

"Yeah," Henry said. "Junior and I had a deal on that painting. We agreed to two million for twenty-five percent of the company."

Frank stared at him. "Funny how things change, ain't it?" He turned to Nigel and gestured toward the painting. "Pack it up."

"Hold on!" Henry said as Nigel took a step forward. "Wait a minute. Let's talk. Look, I don't need six million—never did, really. But if you insist, I'll take the two from the painting plus another two. Total of four million."

Frank considered this for a few seconds, then he nodded. "Four million total."

"And what do you want for it?" Henry asked.

Frank shrugged. "Not much." He paused. "Billy asked for thirty percent for the first two million. I thought that was reasonable, given the risk involved, but for some reason, you agreed to pay only twenty-five."

Henry's eyes narrowed slightly again. "We *both* agreed on twenty-five."

"I understand. Don't get your knickers bunched up. Tell ya what. I'll follow Billy's lead and match his deal. We'll put in the additional two million for an additional twenty-five points. Total of four million for fifty percent of the company." He paused, then he nodded toward Johnny. "And you work your own deal out with your boy's stock options."

Henry looked at him for a moment, then he gave a quick nod. "Done. I'll have my girl draw up the papers."

"Excellent," Frank said, smiling. He turned to Sal. "Mister, looks like you just bought yourself a fine piece of art after all."

"Good," Sal said, his brow furrowed. "In that case, here's the cashier's check." He handed it to Henry.

"Excellent," Frank said. "Bill, give the man his bill of sale."

Sal had his assistant place the painting in a large hardcover case. When it was secure, he said, "Friends, I'm not sure about what just occurred, but if we're all done, we'll go ahead and leave before something else happens."

Danny watched as they exited, painting in hand. He took a quick, deep breath and glanced at Toni.

"What *did* just happen?" she whispered.

Danny leaned over. "Frank Thorne just barged in and took himself from a five-hundred-thousand investment to two-million-five. And he wanted more but for some reason, Henry turned down another two million."

Henry gave Danny a quick smile, a twinkle in his eye.

* * * *

Ten minutes later, Lulu walked into the lobby waving an official-looking printout. "Bank just called. Check's deposited," she said. "And Toni," she added, "your hundred thousand also went in."

Toni nodded.

"Plus," Lulu said, "while I was waiting, I've got the preliminary paperwork for the stock transfer ready for signature."

"Excellent!" Henry said. He turned to Frank. "Thorne, you ready to settle up? There's a little issue of the final two million."

"I am." He nudged Doyle. "Tell Theo and Ernie to come on in."

A minute later, Frank's men entered the office, each carrying two black-leather duffel bags. As soon as they set the bags down on the floor before Frank, one of the men leaned forward, clutching his stomach and groaning.

Frank stared at him. "What'sa matter with Ernie?" he demanded.

"Dunno, boss," the other man said. "He says it was something he ate last night."

Frank gave him a stern look. Then he set two of the bags on Henry's desk before he turned and pointed to the two remaining duffel bags. "We don't need those two. The two of yous take 'em back out to the car and lock them in the trunk. Then stay there. Got it? Don't leave those bags."

"Yeah, got it, boss." The man picked up the bags and started to leave.

"Good. And, Theo, give Ernie a Tums or something."

Frank turned back to the desk, reached down, and unzipped the two cases. "There," he said, looking at Henry. "Two million dollars—cash. A million bucks in each bag. Now you can pay for the generators. Care to count it?"

Danny's breath caught. Each duffel was full to the top with hundred-dollar bills.

"Cash?" Henry said, aghast. "You're bringing two million in cash? Seriously? Are you friggin' insane?"

"No, I am not."

Henry shook his head. "What the hell am I supposed to do with two million in cash? I don't have a big enough army to protect it."

Frank shrugged. "Then, like I said, you should consider counting it. Then maybe you should run it down to the bank before they close early on a Saturday. You'll make their day."

He leaned forward and began signing the ownership-transfer papers.

Henry stared at the cash. He was about to speak when

Luther Rawlins leaned in. "Mr. Cohen," he said, "the Matsumoro limo just pulled up."

Henry said, "All right, then. We'll have to finish this later." He turned to Luther. "I want these two bags in the safe, and then I want you to have a guy—no, two guys—stand guard. Nobody touches the bags, got it?"

Luther nodded. "Yes, sir."

Henry looked at Frank. "Okay, Thorne . . . partner. It's showtime. Let's go get paid."

CHAPTER 29

The Show

Shinichi Tanaka and Koji Nishimura stepped out of the black limousine parked in front of Emerald Fusion Technology and walked into the lobby, where Henry greeted them, a broad smile on his face. "*Ohayō gozaimasu.*" He gave a deep bow to the older of the two men, then he straightened. "Gentlemen! Welcome back to Seattle!"

Shinbone, wearing an expensive navy blue pinstripe suit, with his hair colored silver and tightly slicked back, returned the bow. "Mr. Cohen," he said, smiling and extending his hand. "So good to see you and be back in the Pacific Northwest once again. And on such an auspicious occasion, no?"

Henry nodded. "That it is, sir, that it is. And we're very delighted to have you here."

Shinbone reached for Lulu's hand, smiling. "It's always a pleasure."

"Mr. Ishibashi," she said, smiling, "you are a charmer, as always."

Shinbone beamed. "When I was a young man, maybe. Now, not so much." He paused. "But that's the way of it, no?" He nodded toward Koji, also dressed in a dark blue suit and carrying a large briefcase. "I believe you've met my colleague."

"*Ohayō gozaimasu*," Koji said. He bowed and then shook hands with Henry.

Shinbone turned next to Frank Thorne. "And you must be Mr. McElroy with the James Street fund? Mr. Cohen has said many good things about you."

"Ah, no," Henry said, stepping forward. "We've had a last-minute change of plans. James Street is not here today, sir. Allow me to introduce Mr. Frank Thorne with . . ."

Frank stood up straight. "Thorne Venture Capital. We're new investors."

Shinbone raised his eyebrows. "Oh? I was not aware. I hope all is . . . well?"

Henry nodded. "It's all routine, Mr. Ishibashi. No problem."

Shinbone thought for a second, then he nodded. "Okay." He turned back to Frank. "Mr. Thorne. Very glad to have you here."

After the others were introduced, Henry said, "So, you gentlemen have come a long way. Are you ready for the demonstration?"

Shinbone nodded. "We are. We are very excited. But I suspect the real question is—are *you* ready?" He smiled. "Is LEONARDO ready?"

Henry smiled and clapped his hands together. "LEONAR-

DO 2.0 is ready, bigger and better than ever. And we're anxious to show him to you."

"Excellent!"

"Gentlemen," Lulu said, and then, looking at Toni, "and Ms. Blair . . ." She opened the door to the observation room. "We're ready right this way. If you'd all care to step into the observation room, we'll get started."

****

Lulu pressed a button on the wall inside the observation room. The lights dimmed and the curtains drew open dramatically, revealing the brightly lit lab where Henry stood next to a computer console, facing the group. "Ladies and gentlemen," he said through the overhead speaker, "meet LEONARDO 2.0, our first commercial-scale reactor. Isn't she a beaut?"

"Wow," Toni whispered to Danny. "It's friggin' huge."

Danny nodded. Compared to the first LEONARDO, the latest version was ten times bigger. The domed plexiglass cylinder was a full eight feet tall and three feet in diameter—it dominated the lab. Pale yellow floodlights positioned beneath the cylinder bathed the liquid in a deep amber color that gave an eerie golden accent to the small stream of bubbles coming from the base of the metal reaction cylinder suspended within. Behind the cylinder, a shiny silver cylinder was conspicuously labeled Helium Containment Tank in bright red letters. To the right, the computer control console was manned by four "scientists" in white lab coats. A handful of others hovered around the equipment, clipboards in hand.

"And now," Henry said, "let's show the world what LEONARDO 2.0 can do."

* * * *

Theo sat behind the wheel of Frank's Mercedes and adjusted the radio station. "You okay with Daughtry?" he asked.

Ernie leaned forward, clutching his stomach and moaning softly. "I don't care, bro. I'm hurtin', bad."

Theo looked at him. "Yeah, I believe you. You got the sweats, big time. But you'd better suck it up, dude. Frank will have your ass."

"I'm trying, but I'm afraid things are gettin' critical here. It was those stinkin' oyster shooters last night. They must've been bad." He groaned again. "They're killing me. I'm about to shit buckets all over the inside of Frank's car."

Theo glanced over at him, his eyes wide. "I wouldn't do that."

"I know, but I got it bad, dude." He leaned forward and rested his head on the dash. "This is serious. I can't help it."

Theo stared at him for a moment, then he nodded. "Okay, you're not even allowed to fart in here, never mind so much as put a single turbo stain on one of Frank's seats. He'll kill ya, no questions asked. He'll bury you and the car in the middle of Lake Washington. So I'm gonna do you a favor." He looked around the parking lot. "There ain't no one around here but us two. I'll stand watch. You get your ass inside and take care of business. Then hustle right back on out. But you'd better be back before Frank's done, or it won't matter. He'll kill you anyway. Got it?"

Ernie nodded. "Thanks, man. I owe ya big-time." He bolted from the car, clutching his stomach, and hurried into the Emerald Fusion Technology building.

* * * *

Henry gestured toward LEONARDO 2.0. "We're ready to go," he said, his voice clear through the observation room speaker. "We've been precharging the palladium grid inside the reaction cylinder with hydrogen ions since yesterday afternoon. Now it's time to see what we can do." He turned to the "scientists" at the console. "You guys ready?"

One by one, the technicians reported.

"AC voltage from the outside power plant is alive and ready. Rectifier's on standby."

"Pressure vessel's ready. Compressor's on standby."

"Calorimeter's ready."

"Computer control is up and running."

With the final check-in, Henry said, "Okay, let's go. Start the compressors. Rectifier on, set current to fifty percent power." Almost immediately, an engine in the back of the lab revved up, and a mass of bubbles began streaming from the bottom of LEONARDO 2.0.

"Here we go," Lulu said.

* * * *

Danny watched intently as the process began, and the lab technicians began calling out measurements.

"We've already got fusion!" one of the techs yelled. "Calorimeter's alive. She's generating heat!"

A few moments later, Henry called out, "All readings in the green?"

When all the techs responded in the affirmative, Henry said, "Good. Run us up to seventy-five percent power."

The technician typed in the command, and the noise level increased. The bubbles in the chamber grew more pronounced as the overhead gauges in the observation room confirmed the increase.

"COP's already at 7.0!" a lab tech yelled.

"All right! We're churning out some heat now, boss!" another tech called out excitedly.

Then, suddenly, the lights flickered, and the seats in the observation room gave a pronounced rumble.

Frank gripped the seat rails and looked around. "What the hell was that?"

"Don't worry, Pop," Billy said. "It's routine. Same thing happened last time."

CHAPTER 30

The Rain City Hustle

"Eighty-five percent power now!" Henry called out from the lab.

The woman manning the control panel glanced at Henry with a look of concern. But then she typed in a command. LEONARDO 2.0 began boiling with bubbles at a more rapid pace, steam rising off the surface.

"Wow!" Lulu said excitedly. "Look at that!"

Shinbone grinned widely and clapped his hands together. "Excellent! Just as Myles predicted."

Frank and Billy stared at the chamber, speechless, caught up in the demonstration. Beneath them, their seats rumbled rhythmically—on, then off, then back on again.

"Myles," Lulu called over her microphone, "we're noticing a pretty regular vibration here in the observation room."

From in the lab, Henry glanced back at the windows, then

he looked at the gauges before nodding. "We're good," he said. "It's just the power pulsing." Then he turned to the workers. "Take us to full power!"

The console workers looked at each other, looks of concern on their faces. Neither moved to increase power.

"Full power!" Henry yelled again, more insistent. This time, one of the workers nodded and typed in a command. The noise from the lab quickly reached a crescendo.

A moment later, someone shouted, "There! Look at that sucker go! Right there! We just got a massive temperature spike, boss!"

"10.4 COP!"

"Holy hell," Lulu said, her eyes wide open.

A few seconds later, the rumble in the seats increased at the same moment an alarm began blaring.

A nervous technician looked up. "Caution zone alarm on the pressure chamber, boss! PSI's crossing four hundred!"

"Vent!" Henry ordered. "Now!"

Before anyone could do anything, an overhead pipe burst, and a jet of steam shot out.

"Primary cooling line rupture!"

"Whoa!" one of the workers yelled.

The laboratory Geiger counter immediately went crazy, issuing an almost constant stream of machine-gun-like clicks, clearly audible through the observation room speaker. An automated voice started blaring, "Danger! Radiation breach! Danger! Radiation breach!"

"Radiation?" Henry said. "What the hell?" An instant later,

he yelled, "Shut it down!"

A technician typed in a command, but nothing happened.

"Shut it the hell down!" Henry repeated. "Right now!"

"I sent the command! Nothing's happening!"

"Override!"

The worker pounded frantically on a red switch. "Nothing! No response! We must've fried the controller!"

Suddenly, the walls started to shake, and the seats in the observation room rumbled dramatically.

"What's happening?" Frank said as he leaped to his feet, a look of concern on his face.

The Japanese men also stood.

Lab workers jumped out of their seats, eyes wide.

"It's getting away from us, Myles!" Johnny yelled.

"Cut the input power to the rectifier!" Henry yelled, just as another overhead pipe burst with a loud explosion.

Steam began shooting forth, whistling loudly. A worker in the lab was blown back against the wall as the sound of breaking glass came from inside the lab. Alarms were sounding loudly, first inside the lab, then in the observation room as well. The sign above the observation window announced RADIATION in bright red letters. Yellow and red strobe lights begin to flash.

Henry turned and looked at the lab. "Everyone out! Now! Get 'em out of there! Evacuate the building! Now!"

* * * *

People began running out of the lab and the observation room, meeting in the lobby, where all tried to squeeze through the front door.

"Don't push!" Johnny yelled, directing traffic. "One at a time through the door."

A steady stream of people poured onto the lawn in front of the building.

"Move back!" Johnny shouted a minute later when he finally made it outside. "All the way back to the sidewalk! We're still too close! Danny, help me out here!"

The two men began moving the crowd back into the parking lot, away from the front door.

"What the hell just happened?" Frank demanded when they reached the parking lot and turned back to look at the building. Before anyone could answer, he turned to Billy. "Is this routine, too? Did you have to evacuate the building last time?"

Billy's eyes were open wide as he stared at the smoking building. He said nothing and simply shook his head.

Crashing sounds and the hiss of escaping gasses continued from inside the building for another minute when Lulu suddenly said, "Hey, where's Myles?"

"I saw him running toward his office," someone answered.

Danny scanned the crowd. "Anyone see Myles get out?"

No one answered.

Then someone yelled, "Wait! There he is!"

Henry's shape filled the door. A split second later, a brilliant white flash inside the office was followed immediately by a thunderous blast that literally blew him out the door. He landed facedown on the lawn.

"Myles!" Johnny cried as he, Danny, and the others raced over to him.

Danny reached him first and gently rolled his motionless body over.

"Oh my God!" Lulu screamed.

The skin around Henry's face had been blown off, hanging in charred shreds. His bloodstained lab coat smoldered. He made a weak attempt to lift his hand, but it fell across his chest, motionless, his eyes staring blankly at the sky.

The others looked on. Billy clutched his stomach and retched. Suddenly, a huge plume of flame shot through one of the windows, and steam began pouring out all of the windows.

Danny felt the blast of heat on his back.

"Everyone get back!" he yelled as he jumped up. "C'mon, Jimmy! We gotta get back in case the whole thing goes!"

They raced back over to the pavement, where the Thornes were standing.

"Get away from the building!"

"Is he dead?" Frank yelled.

"I don't know. I think so," Danny said. "It doesn't—"

He was interrupted by the sound of Shinbone and Koji roaring away in their limo, followed a moment later by the rhythmic *thump-thump-thump* of a helicopter hovering overhead. Danny looked up and watched as the black helicopter circled once, then settled to a landing at the edge of the parking lot. Large white letters painted on the side of the chopper spelled out FBI.

* * * *

Three agents wearing black vests bearing the letters FBI jumped out of the chopper, led by Special Agent Ryan Leavitt. They immediately ran toward the group, waving their arms.

"Everybody move away from the building! Farther back!"

As the group shuffled backward, two black Suburbans and two white vans with Department of Energy Emergency Response Team painted on the sides rolled up and skidded to a halt nearby. The doors slid open, and a half-dozen technicians wearing white hazmat suits and carrying Geiger counters poured out of the vans.

Special Agent Leavitt yelled, "We gotta get this damn thing shut down before it blows up half of Bellevue!"

"We're on it!" one of the DOE team members shot back. Most of the team entered the building. Dense gray smoke poured out of the front windows.

Two white-suited figures with red crosses on their sleeves bent to attend Henry. A few moments later, one of the medics shook his head. He pulled out a sheet and covered Henry's motionless body.

From the sidewalk, Lulu sobbed. "Oh, Myles!" she cried.

Toni put her arm around her and comforted her.

Billy and Frank Thorne looked on in stunned silence.

* * * *

Ten minutes later, the DOE team reported that the reactor was shut down and the immediate danger had passed. They were hard at work, setting up a mobile decontamination unit, running DO NOT CROSS tape, and taking measurements with Geiger counters. The FBI agents were just finishing collecting the names and addresses of everyone present when a fully suited-up DOE technician emerged from inside the building.

"It's a Category 4 radiation leak!" he yelled to the agents. "Blown to hell inside. We got tritium readings off the chart and cesium 137 scattered all over! We've gotta seal this place up now!"

"Great," one of the DOE men said with disgust.

"Casualties?" Leavitt yelled.

The man turned and looked as another hazmat-suited technician pointed to the sheet covering Henry. "Just the one, the guy by the door, so far."

Leavitt turned to Johnny. "'No radiation being generated here,'" he mocked. "You guys should've listened to me yesterday. Maybe that man would be alive now. Now look what's happened—one dead, building basically destroyed. I guess it's a little ironic that the victim is Myles Cohen."

"Show some respect!" Johnny yelled.

Special Agent Leavitt turned. "Oh, good. James Albert, you're under arrest for violation of the Atomic Energy Act of 1954. If it's up to me, you're going away for a long, long time, mister. Before they haul you away, I need to know the names of the other owners of this company."

"What?"

"I said I wanna know who else owns this company. I want to

find out who else is responsible for this stupidity. There's gonna be hell to pay."

Johnny quickly glanced at Frank Thorne, their eyes meeting, but then he turned away. He shook his head at Leavitt. "There aren't any other owners. Myles Cohen was the only one."

Leavitt looked skeptical.

"Look it up," Johnny said. "See for yourself."

Leavitt nodded. "We will." He turned to the others. "Okay, then. The rest of you people, it's time for you to leave. Get out of here. This is now a federal restricted area. But remember, we have all your names. And keep this in mind—nothing happened here this morning. If word of this gets out, it will constitute a national security risk, and that's something we take very seriously. Not a word of this goes out to anybody. Forget about it. Don't talk about it. Don't come back. Otherwise, you can expect a long, lonely period of reflection in a federal penitentiary." He shook his finger at the crowd. "So, mum's the word."

"You guys just want the technology for the government!" Johnny yelled, anger in his voice. "You want to steal it!"

Special Agent Leavitt shook his head. "Yeah, right, so we can contaminate some more buildings. Maybe next time, we can blow up a whole city." He turned to an associate and nodded toward Johnny. "Get him out of here. I know a lot of people in Washington who are very anxious to talk to him."

"Fat chance!" Johnny shouted as the agents marched him off to a waiting Suburban.

"The rest of you, go home!" Special Agent Leavitt shouted.

"Hey!" Frank protested. "Wait! I gotta go back inside. My

mon—I mean, my gym bag is inside."

"In there?" A technician laughed as he glanced back at the building. "You can't go in there, buddy. You do, and you'd be dead within fifteen minutes." He nodded toward Henry's covered body. "That man didn't die because of the blast. He died because of radiation poisoning."

"What?" Frank took a step back.

"The radiation in there's off the charts. Don't imagine your gym clothes are worth that."

Frank looked at him, then he looked at the smoking building. "When then? When can I get 'em?"

The technician looked at him for a second, then he turned to another hooded specialist who was approaching.

"Hey, Richie, what's the half-life of cesium 137? I forget."

The technician removed his hood. "Cesium 137? I think it's thirty years, something like that."

The technician laughed and turned back to Frank. "There you go. You hear that? You can pick up your bag in thirty years. That is, if you don't mind digging it out of a hazardous waste dump somewhere."

Frank stared at the men for a second, his mouth open.

"C'mon, Frank," Doyle said a moment later as Special Agent Leavitt eyed the two men suspiciously. "We gotta get out of here."

Frank shook his arm free. "My money's inside!" he hissed.

"I know," Doyle whispered, "and you ain't gonna get it. It's contaminated! Besides, you wanna go to prison for it? C'mon, let's go! The guy's watching us!"

He grabbed Frank and pulled him along.

CHAPTER 31

The Blowoff

Danny hung up his phone and turned to the waiting group. "That was Doc! The Thornes are on 520, headed west at high speed. He'll notify us if they double back."

"Cut!" Murphy yelled as she stepped out of the building.

A second later, the alarms silenced, the warning strobes stopped flashing, and the "steam" and "smoke" pouring from the windows cut off. A cheer went up as everyone stopped in place and started high-fiving each other. The "DOE technicians" started stripping off their hazmat suits, laughing as they did so. Danny, Toni, and Lulu ran over to Henry and pulled the sheet back.

Henry opened his eyes, bright blue beneath the modeling latex "skin" hanging from his face, and propped himself up on an elbow.

"Good. Tell Murph to come get this stuff off my face." He took a deep breath. "I'm getting too old to get launched out of buildings like that."

Everyone returned to the building, laughing and congratulating one another. A minute later, "Special Agent Leavitt" and his "FBI" cohorts returned with Johnny.

"Damn good job, Steve," Henry said. "Almost had *me* convinced." He turned to the group. "Listen up!" he yelled a minute later when he was cleaned up. "Everyone gather around for a second. Grab a beer, except for you guys on the chopper. No beers for you. Besides, you gotta get that thing back to Renton before we have to pay for an extra hour. As for the rest of you, great job, everyone. Best one yet! I'm proud of you all. I want to give a special shoutout to Murphy here and to Kenny Hale for helping us set all this up. It was a doozy."

Everyone cheered. "Hear, hear!"

"We put a thumping to a bad man today, and he won't soon forget it. Now, back to business. First off, Toni, if you'd make sure the painting gets back to Kate Morgan, that'd be great." He nodded toward the parking lot entrance. "For the rest of you, Lulu has the trucks rolling in now. It's all hands on deck. We're gonna blitz through this and cart all this stuff over to the warehouse. Everything goes—we'll sort it out there. You can each pick up your share over there when we're done. But before that, I want to be completely out of here in one hour with the only thing left showing being the FBI's yellow DO NOT CROSS tape. After all, this is a federal disaster area, right? The owner's planning to knock the building down next week, and that will be that. Now let's get this place cleaned up. Johnny's in charge."

As people scattered, Henry turned to Danny.

"You care to meet me in my office?"

* * * *

"Pull up a chair," Henry said. As Danny did, Henry found two shot glasses. He pulled a bottle of Macallan Double Cask from his desk drawer and showed it to Danny. "I been saving this. You a Scotch drinker, Danny?"

"Every now and again."

"Good. This is a good time, then." He filled the glasses and slid one over. "To Harold."

Danny raised his glass. "To Harold."

He sipped the whisky, then set down the glass. "Nice," he said, looking at Henry.

"To your wedding," Henry said, his blue eyes gleaming. "Glad we can get you to the church on time. That's a great woman you've got there, a real keeper."

"Thanks, Henry. Appreciate it." Danny took another sip, then he said, "It went well, didn't it?"

Henry nodded. "Sure did. Right on cue."

"You think Thorne will try to come back on us?" Danny asked.

Henry shrugged. "He may. But the building will be gone—that'll make sense to him with the radiation leak and all. They'll think you're a victim—losing your 401(k) as you did. Nah—I think we're good."

Danny tilted his head and sipped his Scotch. "Funny thing. You know, when Frank Thorne showed up, I was surprised as hell, but *you* didn't seem very surprised. Matter of fact, it seemed like you expected him."

Henry smiled. "What'd I tell you about greedy men?"

"I think you said greedy men are predictable."

Henry smiled. "That's right."

Danny sat up straight. "Makes sense now—you *planned* on him showing up. Thorne just did what you were already expecting. This was never a simple little job to recover a painting for you, was it? You were counting on Thorne crowding in for a big piece the entire time, weren't you?"

Henry held a lighter to the end of a cigar, puffing it until the end glowed bright red. He leaned back, slowly blew the smoke out, and sipped his Scotch. "Well, let's just say we were hoping. We thought there was a pretty good chance that if we set a nice table, a guy like Frank Thorne wouldn't be happy letting a sure thing, a ten-to-one shot get past him. He'd want to make a big score, as big as he could. Show all his friends. We guessed right." He smiled. "But you can't ever tell for sure. Who knows? Maybe it was just our turn to get lucky."

Danny tilted his head, then he chuckled. "Yeah, right. That was probably it."

Henry smiled. "It was a good job, wasn't it? You guys did great, by the way. I know Toni was a little reluctant at first. How's she feel about it now?"

"Well," Danny said, "I don't think you have to worry about her having Logan PI start competing against you, but she's good. Once the Thornes made their move, she came around."

"She was fantastic," Henry said. "Your whole team was. And now, Kate gets the painting back before her old man finds out it was swiped. We get paid. You get paid. Speaking of which, you know, for you guys, the ropers usually get twenty percent of the take. Twenty percent of two-and-a-half million comes to four hundred and fifty grand or so after expenses. Not bad for PI wages. You can pick up most of it when we wrap up here, the rest when Kate gets her new round of funding."

Danny chuckled. "Tempting. But no, that's not what we're in it for. We signed on to get Kate's painting back. She's getting it back. She'll take care of us for that. Anything beyond that is *your* deal."

"Figured you'd say that."

Danny grinned. "But we sure learned a lot."

"Me, too," Henry said, chuckling. "Wanna know the biggest thing I learned? I gotta get me a movie production company! I can't believe I never thought of it. Our ideas and their special effects! Holy hell! Talk about fusion! The look on those guys' faces when the lab blew—damn near perfect! If I had me a Murphy Thompson, there's no tellin' what I could do."

"Well . . ." Danny said. "Ask her."

"I did. She turned me down. Says she likes what she's doing. Plus, I think she's sweet on your boy Kenny."

"Funny how that works."

Danny sipped his Scotch and thought for a couple of seconds, then he said, "So, does it feel better now? I mean, now that you've rung Thorne up?"

Henry puffed on his cigar, then, after a few seconds, he shrugged. "Doesn't bring Harold back so I suppose it's not enough." Then, gradually, a smile formed on his face. "But it's close."

THE FADE

CHAPTER 32

La Ultima Risa

Danny fiddled with the key to the front door of Logan Private Investigations on the first Saturday in October. Three weeks had passed since the big show, and early-autumn weather had turned cooler. The sky over Seattle was streaked with fast-moving low clouds—it would rain soon. He glanced up just as his phone rang. Caller ID flashed the name Toni Blair.

He answered on speaker. "Mrs. Logan, I presume," he said as he opened the door.

"Mr. Logan."

"I have to change your contact info on my phone to Toni Logan," he said.

"You can just say wifey."

"Wifey. That's W-I . . . consider it done."

"Good. On a related topic, I wanted to let you know that I

thought about it, and I've made a decision."

"What? You don't want to change your name to Logan? Or, I get it—you want to hyphenate it. Toni Blair-Logan. Or would it be Toni Logan-Blair?"

"Nope, nothing like that."

"Then . . . ?"

"I wanna go back."

Danny turned the handle of the front door and pushed it open. "What? Back to Toni Blair?"

"No, silly. Back to Hawaii."

"Oh." Danny chuckled. "Like another honeymoon?"

"Yeah, but a *permanent* honeymoon."

"That'd be nice. We've been back for, like, twelve hours and—"

"I know, but I miss it, Danny. The sky's blue. The weather's warm. The beach has actual sand."

"Yeah, well, I think we'd better work on padding our moving fund, then," Danny said. "We're a little light at the moment, and I don't think we can spend our stock in *Fade to Crimson*."

"That's just it," Toni replied. "I've got a good feeling. Kate's going to turn *Crimson* into a big hit. Our share's gonna pay off, and that's how we finance the move."

"You got it all figured out."

"Yeah." She paused. "So, are you there yet?"

"Yep. Just stepped inside. Where are you?"

"I'm crossing 45th. I'll be there in ten minutes. Is there a lot of stuff? How long do you think it'll take us to get through it?"

"You in a hurry?"

"Yeah. I want to get back home and look at our pictures."

Danny smiled. "Hold on, let me get to my office and find out." He walked down the hall and turned into his office. A mound of mail was stacked on his desk. "Yeah," he said. "It's a pretty good pile."

"That's what happens when we get away for two weeks."

Danny nodded as he inspected the pile. "Looks like bills, bills, more bills. Oh, here's a Blake's Harbor postcard from Kate." He flipped it over and quickly read the message on the back.

"Hey!" Toni said. "You should see how much you can get through before I get there."

"And deprive you of the fun of going through all this mail? I don't think so." He put the postcard back in the stack. "I'll wait for you."

* * * *

"What's that?" Toni said.

"It's a thumb drive. It came in an envelope from Lulu. There's a note with it from Henry."

"What's it say?"

"'Danny and Toni,'" he read, "'congratulations again to my two favorite PIs on your wedding! Glad the timing worked out and hope you had a great time in the sun! We were just cleaning up the gear from the Hustle, and Lulu noticed that one of the outside cameras Kenny set up for us recorded to a hard drive. I took a look before she scrubbed the disk, and I found this. Thought you might be interested. Henry.'"

Danny plugged the thumb drive into his computer, and a moment later, his screen filled with an image of the Emerald

Fusion parking lot just as two men walked outside, each carrying a large duffel bag. They placed the bags in the trunk of a black Mercedes before settling in to wait. A minute later, one of the men hopped out and dashed back inside.

"I knew Frank Thorne sent those two outside," Toni said. "I didn't know that one of them came back in."

"Me neither. We must have already been in the observation room by then." They continued to watch and a minute later, Danny suddenly leaned forward. "Wait, who's that?"

A short man approached the Mercedes from the rear, moving quickly across the parking lot, taking care to remain in the driver's blind spot. He walked up behind the driver and then, suddenly, lashed out with his right arm.

"What the . . . ?" Danny said as the driver slumped against the seat. The short man checked the driver's pulse before he leaned through the window. A second later, the trunk popped open. The man turned, walked to the back of the car, and grabbed the two duffels before closing the trunk. Then he quickly strolled away, a duffel bag over each shoulder.

"Was that . . . ?" Toni asked.

"Farley Palmer," Danny said, nodding. "I don't believe it. That was Farley Palmer."

"Play it again," Toni said.

Danny rewound the video. After watching it a second time, he leaned back in his chair and stared at the screen.

"I'll be damned," Toni said. "And wow! That was some split-second timing, right there. If that was Farley Palmer, how'd he manage to be on it like that?"

Danny shook his head. "You got me."

They stared at the frozen figure walking away from the car. "It's almost like he knew," she said. "He–" Suddenly, she paused and turned to Danny. "Wait a minute." She tilted her head. "You don't suppose . . .?" Her voice trailed off, the question hanging in the air.

Danny continued to stare at the screen for another few seconds later, then he shook his head. A smile gradually appeared on his face. "Nah . . . I don't. I think maybe it was just his turn to get lucky."

* * * *

The Pacific Ocean waves thundered onto the beach just south of Todos Santos on the west coast of Baja California in Mexico. A line of pelicans flew south, barely skimming the top of the water while a small flock of seagulls screamed at each other from a cluster of black rocks half covered in seaweed just past the surf. A small grouping of white cumulus clouds stood in stark contrast to the deep-blue sky. Farley Palmer sat on the patio of his small beach home, drinking a Perrier with a slice of lime. He reached into a black leather duffel bag at his feet and pulled out a package. He unwrapped it and set a picture of his wife on the table before him. He took a deep breath, then he smiled.

THE END
(for now)

Acknowledgements

In 1973, the movie *The Sting* was released. Written by David Ward and directed by George Roy Hill, *The Sting* captured the imagination of a young Las Vegas high school student like none before had. It was fun. It was irreverent. It was clever. It was exciting. The good guys (mostly good, anyway) prevailed in the end. I loved it and I wasn't the only one: the film was nominated for ten Academy Awards and won seven of them, including Best Picture, Best Director, and Best Screenplay.

The film made me think—not about learning the art of the con, but instead, about the fantastic world of storytelling—about making something up from a blank page and presenting it to the world. "I can do that!" I said. I started writing short stories (and collecting lots of rejection slips). I wrote my first novel a few short years later (it still sits on a shelf, awaiting revision).

While these first attempts were . . . early, to be sure, the creative passion I'd uncovered for the "art of the story" stuck with me, in large part due to the influences set in motion by *The Sting*. As such, my gratitude goes to all who had a part in the making of this fantastic film! And now, as I make an attempt at paying homage to *The Sting* with *The Rain City Hustle*, if the reader sees any of *The Sting* influences in *The Hustle*, I'm flattered and honored.

I must thank my wife Michelle for her unwavering support on the long path that's led to *The Rain City Hustle*. Quite simply, without her, there's no story.

I'd like to acknowledge my fine team of editors: Molly Sackler, Joyce Lamb, and Peter Senftleben. All authors need a skilled, disciplined team of professionals to reign us in, keep us pointed in the right direction. I'm fortunate—my team is the best!

I worked closely with my excellent cover designer, Pascale Hutton.

I received much welcome encouragement from my beta-reader group as I crafted the early versions of *The Hustle* (that'd be versions fifteen through forty, or thereabouts). Thanks, guys!

Finally, to you, the readers, thank you for sticking with Danny Logan, Toni Blair and the rest of the Logan PI team through the years. Your continued support is wonderful and greatly appreciated.

SIGN UP FOR MY AUTHOR NEWESLETTER

Be the first to learn about M.D. Grayson's new releases and receive exclusive reader content!

WWW.MDGRAYSON.COM

About the Author

Mark (M.D.) Grayson was born in Oakland, California the oldest of five children. His family moved to Las Vegas when he was still very young and it was there that he developed a voracious appetite for reading.

In 2012, he released his debut novel, the self-published mystery *Angel Dance, in* which he introduced the world to Danny Logan and the members of the Logan Private Investigations Agency: Antoinette "Toni" Blair, Joaquin "Doc" Kiahtel, Richard Taylor (the semi-retired previous owner of the agency), and Kenny Hale. *Angel Dance resonated with readers (more than 500 5-star ratings on Amazon) and reviewers alike. Kirkus Reviews said Grayson is "This author is worth watching."*

Grayson followed up on the success of *Angel Dance* over the next three years, releasing new novels in the Danny Logan Mystery Series including *No Way to Die, Isabel's Run, Mona Lisa Eyes,* and *Blue Molly,* all to high acclaim. The stories are set in the Pacific Northwest and the subject matter ranges from murder to the theft of cryptography to child trafficking to drug distribution. In total, the Danny Logan Mystery Series has more than 7,000 ratings on Goodreads (where the average rating is 4.09) and nearly 4,000 ratings on Amazon (the average rating is 4.4 with nearly 2,300 5-star ratings).

Grayson's work has been sold in countries around the world including the USA, Canada, Mexico, United Kingdom, Australia, India, Japan, Germany, France, and others. He lives in Washington state with his wife, Michelle, and two German Shepherds named Otis and Ella.

www.mdgrayson.com

Made in the USA
Coppell, TX
11 December 2022